THE SPIDER:
THE CORPSE BROKER

MASTER OF MEN!
SPIDER ®

THE CORPSE BROKER

By Grant Stockbridge

POPULAR PUBLICATIONS • 2023

CHAPTER 1
WARDS OF DEATH

THE HANDS on the illuminated dial of the Paramount Building clock had almost reached nine-thirty when two inconspicuous street musicians came along West Forty-fourth Street and approached Broadway. The violinist was tall and indefinably foreign-looking; a man with gaunt cheeks and deep, shadowy eyes; with hair that was a trifle long but quite in keeping with the stringy black bow-tie and shabby, eccentric clothing. The other, whose guitar hung from a strap over his right shoulder, was short and thick-set—an Irishman who carried himself rather cockily despite his obvious poverty.

He was in the lead, scarcely able to conceal his impatience as he snaked a way through the laughing sidewalk crowds. "We've been wasting time, Casimir," he exulted. "I knew my hunch was hot. Just look at the mob over here!"

Casimir Belotti obeyed. But his keen, deep-set eyes switched back almost immediately to Garry Burke; and he wondered....

Garry Burke was almost a stranger to him—and certainly *he* was a stranger to Garry Burke. Even had Burke known Richard Wentworth, the wealthy socialite and dilettante criminologist, he never would have recognized, in this seedy-looking fiddler, the man the New York police were hunting to answer a charge of murder. To Garry Burke, Casimir Belotti was just what he appeared to be—a broken-down musician who lived in a squalid

1

tenement and eked out a living by the alms he gathered from passers-by who stopped to listen to his playing.

But Belotti was good. That was what had attracted Burke

to him in the first place and had furnished the inspiration for their partnership.

"A fiddle by itself is an orphan, and a guitar by itself doesn't sound so hot either," Burke had argued when he struck up an acquaintance with Belotti in the stale-smelling hallway of their common rooming-house. "Together, we'll be able to make them stop and listen. What do you say we work double for a while and see how it goes?"

Belotti had shrugged indifferently, and the deal was made. For several days together they had worked the lower East Side streets and bars. Today, Garry Burke had suggested that they take advantage of the big lodge convention that was crowding the city and try their luck in the Broadway district. Belotti had shrugged again—yet now there was no careless indifference in the scrutiny he turned on his companion.

Richard Wentworth was a keen analyst of men, and Garry Burke was not very expert at dissembling. Burke must have some vital reason for wanting to come uptown on this night. His alert eagerness, springy step and probing eyes all betrayed that. Burke was expecting something to happen; and Wentworth's sixth sense told him that the guitarist was not going to be disappointed.

Years of matching his wits against the wiliest of law-breakers, staking his life on his keen understanding of criminals and their methods, had given the Spider an almost uncanny sense of danger, of imminent disaster. Now that instinctive warning sounded in his brain. Something was going to happen... *and then it did!*

They had almost reached Broadway when he caught the roar of the crowd. At first it seemed to be only an excited shout that welled up from the thronged streets. Then, high above the rumbling undertones, rang the cry of terror, the shivery throb of incipient panic!

In an instant the entire side-street, momentarily shocked into silence by that almost animal roar, galvanized into action. With one accord men and women started running toward the corner. Like a sprinter leaving the mark, Garry Burke was with them; was arrowing his way through. Wentworth lost sight of his partner before they had gone fifty feet—and then all thought of Garry Burke was driven from his mind by the turmoil that engulfed him on every side.

BROADWAY HAD become a bedlam; a sea of shouting, screaming men and women who jostled and buffeted one another as they ran wildly in every direction. Police whistles shrilled above the din, automobile horns blared impatiently....

Like an eel Wentworth slipped through the milling crowd until he reached the iron fence behind the police booth in the center of Times Square. Boosting himself up on the railing that separates Broadway and Seventh Avenue, he studied the wild confusion that extended up both streets for many blocks. The jam seemed to be deepest in front of the large motion-picture theaters. Close at hand, an excited throng was just beginning to close in on the entrance of the Paramount. Patrons were streaming out of the theater—indignant citizens who were gasping and holding their noses as they poured out on the street.

"It's an outrage! Where are the police? I want my money

back!" A medley of stormy protests rang in Wentworth's ears even before he crossed Seventh Avenue. But the moment he reached the sidewalk in front of the big theater he realized that this was no ordinary stench-bombing.

The glass windows of the cashier's booth had been shattered, the door at its rear stood open. On the floor, half-spilled into the lobby, lay the body of the pretty, blonde-haired girl cashier. Blood was drenching one side of her face as she tried to get to her knees. The effort was too much for her, and she dropped back, unconscious.

"There was two of them—I saw them do it!" an excited voice screamed at Wentworth's shoulder, as several men stooped to lift the girl. "They smashed the windows and slugged her. Then they cleaned out the cage—two fellers with dark handkerchiefs over their faces. They had guns and—"

"Same thing happened up at the Astor and the Globe," another voice broke in. "I was up there and saw it. I come runnin' down here to get a cop—and here's the same thing! The whole street's bein' stuck up!"

A simultaneous hold-up of Broadway's great cinema palaces—amassing loot that would run into hundreds of thousands of dollars. A hold-up perfectly timed for the hour when the night's receipts had reached almost a maximum, and before the night deposits would begin at the banks....

Wentworth gasped at the brazen daring of such a raid... and in the same instant was knocked off his feet and hurled across the lobby by a tremendous blast!

It had cut down the outpouring patrons by the hundreds

6

and littered the lobby and street with their bodies. For a moment a ghastly, unnatural silence followed that thunderous detonation—then a horrible chorus of agonized screams and dying moans burst from the throats of the mangled victims.

Dazedly Wentworth got to his feet. The ornate theater lobby was a frightful shambles. The entire front had been blown to pieces. Debris was still raining down from the walls and ceilings, burying the twisted, broken forms now trying to drag themselves to safety. A palace of pleasure suddenly transformed into an appalling scene of horror!

The explosion had put an abrupt halt to the exodus from the theater. But suddenly, through that grisly nightmare setting, staggered a figure whose tattered clothing had almost all been torn from his blood-drenched body.

"The manager—they killed him!" he croaked. "They blew up the office—because he wouldn't open the safe. Blew him to pieces...."

Blood gushed from his lips, drowning his words as he pitched forward, fell on his face. Then half a dozen men suddenly rushed over his body—men with felt hats pulled low, dark green handkerchiefs covering the lower part of their faces. They carried bulging satchels and cleared the way with drawn guns.

Three of them flashed through the panic-stricken crowd before the police closed in. The remaining trio seemed to be trapped as the bluecoats came running into the lobby. They bunched, backed away warily, their threatening guns ready.

"Drop those guns or we'll shoot you down!" a red-faced sergeant barked as he lunged forward.

Then something happened—something so strange that it smacked of black magic! Instead of using their weapons, the cornered thugs held out empty, clawing hands—as if to grip their foes by the throat and choke them to death. Those hands were at least fifty feet from the nearest policeman. But suddenly the on-coming cops faltered; their heads went back, and their hands clapped their throats. Their mouths opened wide as they agonizedly gasped for air. Then, one by one, they dropped to the street and lay there, writhing in terrible pain!

Incredulously Wentworth stared at the amazing spectacle. Surely these officers must have been shot, assailed by some concealed weapon… Yet he was certain that the clutching hands of the thugs had been *empty!*

In less than a minute six of the bluecoats were down, their faces turning a ghastly green in death. Three others were on their knees, vainly struggling for breath. That horrible discoloration began to spread over their features. Those who still remained on their feet backed away fearfully.

Through them the green-masked thugs charged, smashing at them savagely with gun muzzles. Eerie terror was even more effective than their weapons. Nobody raised a hand to stop them, and they made a clean getaway—until Wentworth shook off his bewilderment and darted through the fear-paralyzed crowd in pursuit.

INTO FORTY-THIRD STREET he followed them. The side-street was in striking contrast to the avenue. It was almost empty, except for the fleeing thugs—and the dark figure of a woman who suddenly staggered toward Eighth Avenue, a child clutched in her arms.

She seemed oblivious of the masked men until they were almost upon her. Then she whirled, beheld them, went absolutely berserk. She stooped and stretched the child's limp body on the sidewalk—and flung herself at one of the thugs. One hand reached his masking handkerchief, pulled it away; the other clawed wildly at his face.

"Murderer! Bloody murderer!" she screamed. "What did I ever do to you? What did my Bobby ever do to you?"

Viciously the thug swung at her with his automatic, pounded it into her face, over her head… again and again. Her voice rose in a scream of agony, but she clung to him like a leech.

Then Wentworth reached them. The thumb of his left hand pressed against a concealed button in the base of his violin. A portion of the base swung open—revealing an automatic securely held in place beneath the sounding-board. Wentworth grasped it—and the snarling thug received a dose of his own medicine. The second time the blued barrel came down over his skull, he rolled into the gutter.

Quickly Wentworth knelt beside the woman, who had crumpled to the sidewalk and dragged herself to the child. It took only a glance to tell him that she was doomed. Her skull was horribly crushed, and her blood was drenching the street. But she was still conscious.

"I am Ruth Hanley," she gasped. "This is—my Bobby. That murdering beast is Turk Gorman… one of Jigger Monahan's bloody killers. Monahan was there too… I saw him in the crowd outside the theater when I picked up my poor baby. I can't pay him back for this, mister… but you can. Promise me that… swear to heaven you will…."

Suddenly the woman's eyes filled with alarm. She summoned all her remaining strength to push Wentworth aside—just as a shot roared behind him. Turk Gorman had been playing 'possum—taking advantage of Wentworth's absorption. Only the Hanley woman's alertness had saved him from that cowardly bullet in the back.

Wentworth's lips were compressed into a hard, tight line as he fired from the hip. Gorman pitched back into the gutter, a hole drilled through the center of his forehead. This time there was no pretense about his head-long sprawl. But the thugs bullet had caught the woman in the chest.

"Bobby… take care of him…" she gasped, and died.

THE SIGHT of those green-faced policemen, writhing in their death agony, had flashed a quick message to Richard Wentworth's brain. Instantly he had coupled the amazing disaster with two newspaper accounts read during the past week. The accounts had seemed unimportant, though bizarre, at the time. Now he saw them as the preliminary moves of an audacious criminal campaign that would quickly spread mortal terror throughout the city. Hot blood began to pound in his veins.

Richard Wentworth was a hunted fugitive, his life in jeopardy wherever he turned. The Underworld hated him for the aid he had so frequently given Police Commissioner Stanley Kirkpatrick. Any gangland killer would have shot him down without compunction, had his identity as the Spider been revealed. The police sought him for the *slaughter* of more than thirty of

their number. These killings he had tried his best to prevent, but they were chalked up, nevertheless, against him. The police, too, would gladly have put an end to the Spider, even though that Nemesis of criminals had done nothing more than accomplish the tasks at which they had failed. His only hope of survival lay in this identity of Casimir Belotti, which he had assumed….

The sight of those dying policemen, ruthlessly cut down in the performance of their duty; Ruth Hanley, lying there in a pool of her own blood a few short minutes after she had been sitting in a theater with her baby—these things sounded a challenge that he could not resist. The plea of the helpless, the appeal of the ruthlessly down-trodden, the flaunting defiance of the heedless lawbreaker to whom human suffering and human life meant nothing—those were the things to which he responded automatically….

SWIFTLY WENTWORTH glanced up and down the street. The dead thug's companions had fled, and the sound of the shots had attracted no attention in this night of bedlam. Out of his pocket he took a small silver cigarette lighter. For an instant he bent over the fallen man, pressed the bottom of the lighter against the fellow's forehead. When it came away the crimson replica of a spider was imprinted.

The crimson seal of the Spider! A warning to this thieving killer's master that, even though he might hamstring the police, an implacable avenger was now on his trail!

From the dead thug Wentworth turned to the unconscious child. Little Bobby Hanley's heart was still beating regularly, but his attempts to bring the boy back to consciousness were unavailing. That was a task for a doctor.

Wentworth picked up the little body, cradled it in his arms. Before he had gone a dozen paces, a car came toward him from across Seventh Avenue. A large sedan with a uniformed chauffeur at the wheel and a single occupant in the rear. With the unconscious child held up to stress his need, Wentworth stepped out into the street and hailed the machine—then stepped back just in time as the man in the rear leaned forward and ordered his driver to go on!

For an instant Wentworth stared after the disappearing sedan, and the face of its occupant was etched indelibly on his memory. A high-boned, gaunt-cheeked face with a prominent nose and bushy gray brows; the face of an aesthete—or of an inhuman devil. A face that was strangely familiar, and yet one that Wentworth knew was not numbered among his acquaintances....

Suddenly memory flashed out of his subconscious, and he had it! He had glimpsed that face only a few minutes before, as he ran across Broadway. The man had been standing beside the police booth, grinning like a satyr as he watched the turbulent excitement all around him. And now had his chauffeur drive him right past the half-demolished theater so that he might obtain a close-up view of the incredible havoc the thieves had wrought?

That striking countenance was stark in Wentworth's mind's eye as he circled the terrible, body-littered sidewalk in front of the Paramount. He walked up Broadway with his limp burden in his arms, looking for a taxi or a car that he could commandeer. But he was not the only one with such a mission. The street was filled with injured people—and with dead policemen.

At the Mayfair, the Hollywood, the Capitol—all the large picture houses were the same. Ambulances were lined up at the curb. Helpless interns worked over rows of policemen whose agonized faces had turned a horrible, putrescent green—men for whom doctors and ambulances could do nothing more. Some were men whom Wentworth knew; who had stood staunchly beside him and Kirkpatrick in their battles with the lawless....

Before he reached Fifty-seventh Street and found a cab, Wentworth realized how deeply this grisly horror had sunk its talons into the heart of New York. A murder-mad criminal had thrown off all restraint and was running amok in the metropolis. The Spider's tense fingers itched for the combat....

"They will pay for what they did to you and your mother, Bobby—for what they did to all those others!" he softly promised the limp form in his arms; and his grim-lipped face at that moment was not a pleasant thing to behold.

CHAPTER 2
SLAUGHTER NIGHT

RICHARD WENTWORTH speedily solved the problem of medical attention for little Bobby. On East Ninetieth Street was an old German physician who could give the six-year-old the best care. This medico felt himself to be under great obligation to Wentworth and would do anything to repay the man who had once snatched him from the clutches of merciless killers.

Wentworth gave the driver Dr. Hugo Schoenheit's address, then sat back to reconstruct the first manifestations of this strange *discoloring* death that had swept Broadway.

About a week ago Belle Seeley, the musical-comedy star, had been returning to her apartment with an escort, when two masked men confronted them. The escort put up a battle and managed to yell for the police before being knocked out. A patrolman answered that call, but, according to the testimony of the actress, he suddenly stopped as he came running toward them—then fell to the street, gasping for breath and writhing in terrible convulsions.

The hold-up men paid no attention to him. They stripped her of her jewels and made a leisurely, confident departure. When help finally arrived, the policeman was dead and his face was a ghastly, mottled green—the result of a heart attack, the medical examiner had declared.

That was the first time the Green Death had made the columns of the New York newspapers. The next was two days later, when Sam Trepman, a wealthy financier, was held up and robbed in his own home. Trepman managed to touch off a burglar alarm, and a radio car answered. The officers arrived as the thugs were looting the financier's safe. But one of them dropped to the steps as he came running up the front stoop. The other barely got out of the car before he pitched to the sidewalk and lay squirming in horrible agony.

"Those crooks seemed to realize that this would happen," Trepman had told the newspapermen. "They didn't even try to run when the radio car arrived. One of them turned on me and said, 'So what good did that do you, smart guy?' and then he hit me over the head with his gun."

Again the medical examiner had pronounced the deaths the result of heart attacks and had grimly stuck to that diagnosis when the newspapers began heckling him. But tonight, there were nearly a hundred more police deaths to be explained—a hundred cases of heart failure which all occurred simultaneously?

"Looks like trouble ahead there, boss." The driver interrupted Wentworth's thoughts as the cab slowed.

The taxi, running north on Third Avenue, had just passed Eighty-fifth Street—and was approaching Eighty-sixth. Wentworth peered through the window and saw that the street ahead was swarming with people who ran wildly in every direction. Then he caught the unmistakable chatter of a sub-machine gun! Screams of terror shrieked into the night!

By now the cab had reached the corner—and things began to happen with lightning rapidity.

RICHARD WENTWORTH •

Out of the stampeding crowd a blue-coated figure came running, to leap upon the running-board, yank the door open.

"Pile out! Gotta have this cab!" he barked. "We can't wait for ambulances, with hundreds—"

The words died on his lips as his eyes widened in sudden fear. His hand darted to his throat. Strangling gasps tore from him as he lost his grip, tottered backward. And as he fell to the street, the illumination from an arc-light revealed his contorted face already turning a sickly, fatal green.

Yorkville was in pandemonium. As the taxi slithered to a stop, Wentworth gazed out on what looked like the street of a European city where an attempted revolution had just been mercilessly suppressed. Gay Eighty-sixth Street, lined from Third to Second Avenue with German-American restaurants and nightclubs, was a shambles. The sidewalks and roadway were littered with bodies; prone figures that tried feebly to crawl... others that lay ominously still. Everyone who could run was fleeing as if from a plague spot. And among those who leaped into waiting cars, Wentworth glimpsed a score of green-hand-kerchief-masked thugs.

With a final burst of machine-gun lead that hosed the buildings on both sides of the street warningly, the crooks' cars got underway, ruthlessly riding over the prostrate victims.

Wentworth was inundated by the wounded and dying. Some half-carried by their friends, others crawling on hands and knees, they closed in on the cab, begging to be taken to a hospital.

"I can go the rest of the way on foot." He thrust a five-dollar

CASIMIR BELOTTI

bill into the driver's hand. "Take as many of them as you can and rush them to a hospital. Then, for God's sake, come back here for more!"

WITH BOBBY HANLEY in his arms, he stepped out into that stricken bedlam, turning horrified eyes from the scenes that greeted him on every side. Men, women and children had been cut down indiscriminately by that savage tommy-gun fire.

"They raided the whole block," one ashen-faced man muttered, his voice so low that he might have been talking to himself. "We were in Meyer's when it happened. They came in and lined us all up and took everything we had. But that was only the beginning. That wouldn't have been so bad. It was when we tried to get away that hell broke loose. They had both ends of the street blockaded, and somebody must have got panicky— somebody started shouting and tried to break a way through them. That was when the machine-guns opened up. God in heaven—it doesn't seem possible!" he groaned. "Our wedding anniversary. Only a few minutes ago we were laughing and singing in there, and now this…."

Not until then did Wentworth glimpse the bloodied corpse of the woman that lay huddled in the doorway behind him….

From end to end the machine-guns had turned that festive, crowded street into a shocking nightmare. Poignant tragedy confronted Wentworth wherever he turned; and as he passed among the moaning victims, the wailing bereaved ones, he grimly swore anew that the monster who was responsible for this wanton slaughter of innocent people should pay for his atrocious crimes.

The fiendish monster who was responsible… Had Wentworth been ready to accept Ruth Hanley's implication and lay the responsibility for the crimes at the door of Jigger Monahan, this uptown raid would have convinced him of his mistake. Monahan was a typical gang leader, a man of limited vision and small power. He was utterly incapable of conceiving and setting on foot a campaign of this diabolical magnitude, and his organization was not nearly large enough to have staged both the Times Square and Yorkville massacres.

Jigger Monahan was a tool, nothing more—just as another tool must have been used to perpetrate this outrage. Bloodthirsty, conscienceless tools in the hands of a super-criminal….

Suddenly Wentworth stared. Coming toward him was the aesthetic-looking man he had seen in the rear of the sedan in Times Square; the same high-boned, gaunt-cheeked face, prominent nose, longish gray hair. There could be no mistake! Wentworth even recognized the suit the oldster wore.

But now that striking face was shocked and filled with horror. The old man had just come out of one of the larger restaurants, and he stared about him with compassionate, unbelieving eyes. At his side was a pretty, blonde-haired young woman who took his arm as they stepped out onto the sidewalk and started toward Third Avenue. Within inches of Wentworth they passed; so close that his glance momentarily locked with the old man's and not a spark of recognition flared in that unmistakable countenance….

Incredulously Wentworth stared after them. The same man at the scene of both tragedies that night… and yet regarding them with attitudes so different… What was the fellow—a master actor, a Machiavellian fiend come to gloat over the misery his puppets caused?

Could he be the fiend who had forged this weapon of the Green Death?

A few minutes later Wentworth rang Dr. Schoenheit's bell and stood under the hall light while the grizzled old physician regarded him curiously.

"This little fellow was hurt in an explosion; he's been like this nearly half an hour," he explained quickly. "Richard Wentworth sent me here with him to ask—"

But he got no farther. The mention of his name acted like a magic talisman. Instantly Schoenheit stepped forward and took the boy from his arms, hurried with him to a little laboratory at the rear of the building. Swiftly he went to work, while the foreign-looking violin player sketched what had happened to the child.

"The respiration—it is good. The heart—it is regular and not too weak," Schoenheit nodded satisfiedly. "He will be much better in a little while." Shrewdly his gray eyes searched his visitor's face. "If it happens that you should see Mr. Wentworth, tell him it will be all right with the boy," he nodded again significantly. "I will do everything for him—everything."

Bobby Hanley could be in no better hands, Wentworth knew; and the knowledge gave him a feeling of relief as he left the house. Now he was free again. His thoughts flashed back to the tragedies of the night. He recalled Garry Burke's tenseness, expectancy; his conviction that Burke had led the way to Times Square, purposely, expecting something to happen.

What had become of the guitar player in that tumult, he wondered… and decided to investigate as soon as he reached their rooming-house.

THAT SHABBY, ancient tenement was located on a dingy, noisome canyon of a street below Stuyvesant Square and east of the Bowery; a section of New York's old East Side that had defied the best efforts of all the city's slum-clearance campaigns. Like its squalid neighbors, it was grimy and battered looking, its fire-escapes piled high with rubbish and household impediments of every sort, its stale-smelling hallway still feebly gas-lit.

None of the street-corner loungers gave a second glance to the down-at-the-heels fiddler as he stalked to the gloomy, cave-like entrance. His kind were not unfamiliar in that rabbit warren of humanity; they came and went, managing somehow to keep body and soul together until they dropped out of sight entirely. But Wentworth eyed them keenly as he passed. He noticed that they were not nearly so numerous as usual, for this hour of night. Familiar figures among them were missing… on business' uptown?

Leaving his violin and bow in the stuffy little cell of a room that was Casimir Belotti's home, he climbed two flights higher to Burke's doorway. Just as he was about to rap his knuckles on the paint-blistered panel he tensed, hand in mid-air. His keen ears told him that Garry Burke was not alone.

Came the sounds of a scuffle, a fist slapping viciously against flesh—something heavy thudding to the floor. Then the growl of low, venomous curses.

"Try that again, you lug!" a thick voice rasped. "Next time—"

But Wentworth did not wait to hear what would happen next time. Noiselessly he hurried along the hallway and up two more flights of steps to the roof. Here he cat-footed to the yawning mouth of an air-shaft and reached inside to where a thin, tough strand of silken rope dangled from a pulley set in the shaft's rim. That almost invisible strand of the Spider's web had been placed in position there to serve as a means of quick exit from his own room, should the necessity arise.

Wentworth tied one end around his waist, grasped the rope in both hands, let himself over the edge carefully. Past the upper floor he lowered himself... and again heard the soft mutter of muted voices from the floor below. Now he knew that Garry Burke was in danger; that death hovered close over him....

Cautiously he kneed the side of the shaft, as he reached Burke's floor. His feet found the ledge of the air-shaft window and he drew himself up close to it. His body was against the panes. They were grimy and partly covered with a translucent window paper, but the stuff had peeled away at the edges so that he could peer through into the room.

Garry Burke sat there helplessly, covered by the ready guns of two thugs who stood on either side of him. A third bent over him with clenched fists. Blood streamed from Burke's nose and from a cut in his upper lip. But his eyes were defiant and his jaws were grimly clenched. His pockets, Wentworth noticed, were turned inside out—their contents dumped on the kitchen table.

"So you're not gonna talk, eh?" one thug snarled. "Ain't that nice? You're not gonna tell us what you're doin' with this in your pocket!"

He held something up before Burke's eyes. As the light fell upon it, Wentworth saw that it was a patch of human skin several inches square! A patch of skin on which the crimson seal of the Spider had been stamped!

"So you don't know nothin' about the Spider, but you go around cuttin' his mark off o' stiffs," the thug sneered. "Maybe this'll learn you how to talk!"

Murder gleamed in his eyes as his right hand whipped an automatic from his hip pocket. But before he could smash the barrel down into Burke's face, there came a startling interruption. Suddenly the air-shaft window crashed in—and through it hurtled a hunched figure.

That leap carried Wentworth all the way to the would-be murderer, and his arms closed firmly around the fellow's waist—sent him sprawling backward. The automatic dropped from his fingers and clattered across the room as Wentworth's fist smashed savagely into the snarling face. Clutched in each other's arms, they rolled and threshed in a grim death struggle.

The momentary astonishment of that amazing interruption was all that Garry Burke needed. He threw himself forward in a leap that up-ended the table. When he scrambled to his feet, the table was gripped in both his hands—smashing down onto one of his opponents. The gunman's bullets tore through the wood.

That thug toppled in a heap, as the table-edge split his skull. Burke whirled, just as a bullet whistled past his ear. The second killer was eyeing him wolfishly, finger pressing back on the trigger. Then a body swept up from the floor, crashed into him. It was his fallen mate, clutched in Wentworth's steely fingers—smashed into him even as Wentworth's relentless grip snapped the neck with a swift, head-over-heels *jiu-jitsu* hold that ended his own struggle.

The swift death of two of his companions was too much for the surviving gangster. The fear of death was upon him as he scrambled to his feet, triggered blindly and dashed toward the door. Yanking it open, he dived out into the hallway.

TWO OF the thugs were dead but the third one was free to speed word to his chief, Jigger Monahan, and bring the rest of the gang swarming back. Burke realized that. His eyes were grim as he snatched up the gun that had fallen from Wentworth's opponent's hand, and backed away from the door. Wentworth was at his side in an instant.

"The roof!" he snapped. "We can't stay here now."

That floor of the hall was still empty when he reached the door and peered out. A rumble of voices came from downstairs, the voices of men who had not yet mustered sufficient courage to come up and investigate. Leaving the corpses where they had fallen, he and Burke ran out into the hallway and up the two flights to the dark roof. Across five of the adjoining roofs they hurried, then down through a roof-house into the corner building.

By the time they reached the sidewalk, they caught sight of several dark figures converging meaningfully on the rooming-house. Jigger Monahan's yeggmen had arrived even before the police were notified—but too late. Wentworth and Burke turned down a side-street and headed for a Bowery lodging-house where Jigger and his henchmen would never think to look for them.

There Wentworth faced his companion inquiringly.

"You sure saved my bacon that time, Casimir," Burke admitted, as he sat back and mopped his brow. "I sure thought my number was up when that rat started at me with his gun. It looked mighty bad for little Jimmy—"

He caught himself up short, hesitated for a moment—then a quizzical half-smile came over his features.

"After what you just did for me, I guess maybe I better come clean with you, Casimir," he confessed. "I knew those yeggs trailed me from Times Square. They saw me slice that spider stamp off the forehead of a dead crook and started after me. But I thought I had given them the slip. I found out different when they cornered me in my room."

"But that curious spider stamp—why did you want that?" Wentworth questioned with well-simulated puzzlement.

"Because that's the mark of the Spider, the super-criminal—the man I am down here in the slums trying to find," Burke grinned. "There isn't any Garry Burke that I know of, Casimir. Your side-kick's been holding out on you. I am really Jim

Mack, a dick attached to the acting police commissioner's office. Sanford Dane is convinced that the Spider is hiding out somewhere down here on the East Side, and he'd give his eye teeth to get his hands on that same Spider—which is the reason for my assignment.

"At first I thought Dane was all wet, but now I know that I'm on the right track. The Spider is the man behind this Green Death we saw all over Broadway tonight. He was there in Times Square and was responsible for all that hell—"

"But why, if he is the Green Death leader who protected the robbers—why would he kill one of them and put that stamp on his face?" Wentworth asked.

"That was just a warning," Jim Mack answered readily. "Just an act of terrorism—an object-lesson to put the fear of the devil into the rest of his rabble. This yegg Gorman must have done something to cross the big-shot—so he got his and the spider mark was stamped on his forehead as a warning to the rest. The Spider figures to have every yegg in town knuckling down to him. But I put a crimp in that by slicing the mark off.

"I'm on a hot trail now, Casimir." He leaned forward earnestly. "And on account of what you did for me tonight, I'm going to let you in on it with me. Give me a hand, and we'll nab the Spider—and split the juicy rewards Sanford Dane and the D.A. are offering for his capture. Dead or alive, it doesn't make any difference—as long as we land him. From what I've got on him now that's going to be a cinch!"

In his eagerness he stretched out—and before he could

answer Richard Wentworth's fingers were grasped and he was shaking hands on the bargain for his own apprehension!

CHAPTER 3
REIGN OF TERROR

THE STORY of the Broadway and Yorkville holdup raids was emblazoned on the front page of every New York newspaper the next morning—the "Green Death" on every tongue. More than a hundred and fifty policemen had been stricken by the inexplicable seizures—and in every case the victim had died despite all attempts to save him.

Put to rout by a barrage of unanswerable questions, the medical examiner, no longer daring to attempt to dismiss the fatalities as heart attacks, had refused to speak for publication. But the shocked city knew that the Green Death was just that… certain death for anyone gripped by it. The police were powerless to protect even themselves!

The effect of that realization on the denizens of the Underworld was immediate, unmistakable. A new confidence asserted itself in the slums—renewed truculence on the part of even the youngest hoodlums. Crime had found a champion and was quick to throw off the subservience to authority which had held it in check.

The first day was marked only by petty holdups, by street brawls, by sneering remarks as policemen went by on their rounds. But Wentworth quickly recognized the signs of a growing recklessness that was sure to be the precursor to an outbreak of utter lawlessness. The seeds of the whirlwind had been sewn… and already the wild crop was sprouting.

"Life and property won't be worth a damn in this town in a couple of days, if this keeps up," Jim Mack worried, as he and Wentworth made their round that day, stopping in saloons and wherever it was likely that they might pick up a chance remark that would put them on the trail of their quarry. "The Spider is mighty clever—don't make any mistake about that. He covers his tracks beautifully. But they all make mistakes—and he made a damn bad one last night in Times Square."

On Wentworth's urging, Mack had made up his face so that he would not be so readily recognizable should they encounter the thug who had escaped from Mack's room. But they met no difficulties that day—nor did they pick up anything of value. The Underworld was seething, but its denizens were guarding their tongues with unusual care….

Jim Mack's prognostication was borne out that very night. This time he was not able to stumble onto a lead that would take them to the scenes of the proposed crimes. But in the morning Wentworth learned that once more lawlessness had run wild; the shadow of the Green Death had fallen blightingly on all who tried to interfere. Three banks had been broken into, their night depositories looted; two large hotels had been held up and fine-combed by bands of thieves; half a dozen wealthy citizens had been robbed in their homes. And whenever the police had responded, they had crumpled up and died at the first sign of opposition….

Those newspaper accounts served as the match that ignited

the wholesale conflagration. Encouraged by this new immunity to punishment, flagrant lawlessness began to spread like wildfire.

The moment Wentworth and Mack left their Bowery dwelling that morning they sensed the unrest all around them. In the eyes of even the most shiftless and broken-spirited derelicts there was now a predatory gleam. Before noon the radio was broadcasting accounts of daring hold-ups and robberies in widely scattered parts of the city.

With gleaming eyes the saloon habitues listened to those announcements. But their guarded comments were in such low tones that Wentworth could pick up nothing—until he and Jim Mack found themselves in a fetid-smelling hole-in-the-wall bar on a side street off First Avenue. They were in the middle of a rendition of *The Sidewalks of New York* when the bartender cocked his ear to the low-tuned radio behind him.

"Can that racket for a while," he ordered, as he spun the volume control knob and brought the station in clearly.

"The crime wave which has swept New York City for the past forty-eight hours reached a new point of boldness this morning in a daring daylight hold-up of the Fifth Avenue jewelry store of Gilvany and Sons," the voice of the announcer filled the bar. "The thieves made a clean sweep of jewelry and precious stones valued at nearly two hundred thousand dollars. And once more the police reserves, who responded to the store's holdup alarm, were stricken with the inexplicable Green Death as soon as they had crossed the threshold."

The radio voice went on to supply more details, but Wentworth was no longer listening. Standing at the bar, a glass of

beer raised to his lips, his gaze
was focused across the imita-
tion mahogany to where two
other customers leaned against
the counter. The eyes of one
had opened appreciatively, as
he listened to the announcement. The other had shrugged,
grimaced deprecatingly—and now was speaking. Keenly Wentworth watched his lips, reading the words.

"Pretty good, yeah—but wait till tonight," the fellow
muttered. "We'll show them something. We'll pull a haul that'll
make that stick-up look like a kid's job. Stores is all right, but
warehouses—that's where you make a haul. Wait till we—"

Now his companion was interrupting with a question. Wentworth tensed and scanned the rim of his glass.

"Yeah, we can use a few more good men," came the answer.
"I won't be able to take you down myself, but you can tell Joe
Horeski I sent you, in case I'm not there when you come. That'll
do—just tell Joe that Socker Lewis sent you, and it'll be all right.
Eight o'clock's the time—in Benny Manno's garage. I'll see you
there—may be there before you show up."

There was more; but Wentworth caught the Seeker's suspicious, penetrating eyes turned in his direction. He did not dare
wait longer. Picking up his violin, he nodded to Jim Mack and
made a new start on *The Sidewalks of New York*—but now his
nerves were tingling, and his thoughts were far from the music
which poured from his instrument.

This warehouse hold-up was to be somewhere on the West

Side; that much he had gathered. And the leader of the raiding party evidently was to be Joe Horeski, a surly ex-pugilist who had recruited a gang of thugs whom he ruled by sheer brawn. Monahan and Horeski made two gang leaders who were taking part in this wave of crime, and the one who had perpetrated the Yorkville raid made three… One after the other the wielder of the Green Death was lining up the Underworld chieftains and enlisting them in his campaign. But at last Wentworth had a means of contacting the fellow. Socker Lewis little suspected it, but he was sending not one but *three* new recruits to Joe Horeski that night….

AS SOON as they were out of the bar, Wentworth outlined to Jim Mack what he had overheard; imparted the information in such a manner that Mack could not fail to catch its significance. The detective's eyes sparkled with excitement, and he whistled softly.

"You've got something there, Casimir," he said admiringly. "It'll be dangerous—but we're going to invite ourselves to that party. We'll be guests of Mr. Socker Lewis's. The only trouble," he said, "is what we'll do when he shows up. That may prove sort of embarrassing."

"Not if this Socker does not 'show up,' it won't," Wentworth pointed out—and again Jim Mack eyed his strange partner with new respect….

On one side of Benny Manno's garage an alleyway ran around to the rear. On the other was a boarded-up tenement house with an areaway cellar entrance beneath the doorway. By a little past seven that night Jim Mack was posted behind an ash barrel and

31

a heap of rubbish at the entrance to the alley; Casimir Belotti was hidden in the waste-paper littered pit of the areaway. For half an hour they maintained their watch—then Wentworth tensed and stared keenly down the block.

Socker Lewis was coming—approaching the garage from *his* end of the block. And he was alone—which would make things easy.

Wentworth waited until the crook was abreast of his hiding place—then he leaped. In a split-second his gun barrel came down over Lewis' head. He caught the man in his arms, then thrust the inert body over the railing, dropped it into the pit. Wentworth swiftly followed, picked up the unconscious form; dragged it through the cellar doorway that he had already pried open. Once inside, he quickly bound and gagged the fellow securely. He rejoined Jim Mack—the first job well done.

Joe Horeski was the second problem.

Wentworth and Mack walked into the garage confidently and were escorted into a large back room by Benny Manno. There Horeski and a dozen of his men awaited them—hard-eyed individuals who regarded the newcomers with little satisfaction:

"Socker Lewis sent you?" Horeski thrust his bullet head forward and repeated their introduction sneeringly, as if to challenge its authenticity. "Well, you look like you might have some guts," he said to Mack. "But why'n hell does he send me a guy like this?"

His little pig-eyes gleaming, Horeski strode forward as if to tread the ill-favored recruit underfoot. Wentworth stood there in apparent helplessness, watched him come. But just before the bruiser reached him, his hand suddenly streaked to his shoulder—and Horeski stared down dumbly at the automatic muzzle now no more than an inch from his belly.

"In my country we are taught to use weapons expertly," Wentworth said softly. "If you would care for a demonstration...."

The gang chief backed away, a sickly grin on his ring-scarred face. "That's what I wanted to know," he growled. "I know you're okay else Socker wouldn't of sent you. But I got to test my men myself."

They were apparently accepted, although Wentworth realized that Horeski had no liking for them. They were to be tolerated but not trusted. Yet, curiously, these crooks did not hesitate to accept them as partners on a mission that would be fraught with danger. It was characteristic—they were that supremely confident, brazenly indifferent, about what lay before them.

This was no usual gang of thieves embarking on a perilous raid; they were more like ordinary workmen going out on a job. There was nothing to fear from the police....

Eighteen formed the raiding party that left the garage. Wentworth noted that when it was time to take to the trucks he and Mack were separated. With four of the thugs, he took his place in a big truck that rolled out into the street and headed westward. His instructions were of the scantiest.

"There won't be nothing to this," Horeski had said. "A couple o' watchmen to take care of—that's all. Then all you gotta do is get the stuff into the trucks and get goin'. Don't worry about the cops—they've been fixed!" He winked.

The place to be looted was a fur warehouse. Mack, Wentworth

The Spider leaped into action—his guns blazing twin streams of death!

knew, had hoped to learn its location so that he could notify the police and bring help. But something about Horeski's contempt for interference convinced him that police would be of no assistance. If the master of the Green Death was to be brought to justice, it was up to the Spider to accomplish it, single-handed....

THE TRUCK finally came to a halt on West Thirty-sixth Street, beyond Eighth Avenue. The big warehouse loomed dark and silent beside it, as somber and lifeless as the deserted street.

Evidently the watchmen had already been "fixed"—for now a great steel door rolled upward, almost noiselessly, from the sidewalk. The truck turned in, rolled down a ramp and backed up against a loading platform. Two others were already in position when Wentworth's truck arrived, and a fourth made its appearance a few moments later.

That made the raiding party complete—and already the heavy bales of valuable furs were beginning to flow down to the loading platform. Wentworth stepped out to take his place with the others, but the moment he sprang onto the platform he tensed. From the interior of the building came the bark of shots, the sound of yelling voices!

With one accord the thieves whirled and darted inside, Wentworth close at their heels. Just beyond the loading platform doorway, he almost tripped over the body of the watchman, sprawled in a pool of blood. In the little shipping office beyond another man slumped over a desk, his skull smashed.

Now the bark of shots was louder, and with them came the rasp of savage curses. Somebody was giving a good account of himself—and even before Wentworth reached the upper floor he knew who he would find there.

Jim Mack! The detective evidently had managed to evade the others long enough to reach the main office, reach a telephone and put through a call to the police!

The glass panels of the office wall were shattering to fragments as Wentworth leaped to the rescue. But he was too late. Two of the thugs lay sprawled in the big room behind the office; the others swarmed through the doorway, closed in upon Mack, relentlessly. For an instant he fought them off from behind the shelter of a safe; then the telephone dropped from his hand, clattering to the floor as he fell.

"Never mind that!" Horeski roared, as he sent his men back to their task. "He called the cops—so what? The hell with them! Get back on the job and put those furs on the trucks!"

In a few moments his curses and threatening fists had cleared the office—of all save the figure that slipped quietly into a corner beside a filing cabinet.

As soon as Horeski's bellowing voice faded in the distance, Wentworth stepped out into the darkened office and groped his way to Jim Mack's side. His pocket flashlight played over the detective's blood-covered face. When his fingers slipped beneath Mack's coat they found the heart still beating. Mack was alive; unconscious from what appeared nothing more than a glancing bullet that had laid open his scalp.

Mack was alive, but had already summoned his mates to their doom! If the lives of those policemen were to be saved, only the Spider could save them! One against more than a dozen of the gangsters—what chance was there?

QUICKLY WENTWORTH slipped into a chair behind a flat-topped desk and propped up the flashlight so that it played directly upon his features. From a pocket in the lining of his coat came a small, compact make-up kit, a little metal mirror. Swiftly his adept fingers went to work—and with incredible speed the countenance of Casimir Belotti began to disappear, transformed into a hideous mask.

The skin became sallow, puckered into deep, ugly wrinkles;

the nose was beaked and predatory; lips disappeared entirely, until the mouth was nothing more than an almost colorless gash revealing stained, fang-like teeth. Into his eyes went drops that made them glisten; over his eyebrows tufts of shaggy hair. He adjusted a long, matted black wig.

From inside the lining of his vest Wentworth produced two black objects. One he poked up into a wide, floppy brimmed black felt hat. The other he shook out into a long black cape that covered him almost to his shoe tops. Clothed in that somber garb, two automatics firmly clutched, the twisted, hunched figure of the Spider now glided out of the bullet-scarred office toward the crowded loading platform.

The thieves were toiling like beavers when that sinister figure came upon them. In two steady streams, the wealth of fur was pouring into the waiting trucks… Suddenly the smooth precision of the looters was shattered by a maniacal cackle of a laughter that grated discordantly on their nerves, struck terror into their hearts. With that eerie howl rising from his twisted lips, the Spider leaped into action. His guns blazed twin fires of death as he threw himself upon the mobsters.

Three went down, trying to shoot back. Half a dozen others whirled, grabbed for their guns. But the weaving, bouncing figure that bore down upon them seemed to offer no mark whatever. Their guns roared harmlessly, and the realization of their own futility added to the panic that had seized them.

"The Spider!" one howled in stark terror. He flung himself headlong toward the loading platform doorway, and after him went a mad stampede.

The Spider showed them no mercy—just as he knew they would show the police no mercy once the officers arrived. Four dropped in their tracks before he reached the doorway. He hesitated momentarily, prepared to meet the storm

of lead that would greet him the instant he charged through that portal. Then what he had feared, happened.

The police arrived!

The shrill scream of their sirens struck cold fear into his heart; not fear for himself but for *them*. Crouching low, he flung himself through the doorway in a crazy lunge. Even as he sprang out onto the platform, he saw that it was too late. Two of the loaded trucks were just about to roar off into the night, when the bluecoats swarmed in. Desperately the policemen tried to block that escape. Up onto the running-boards they leaped, clutched at the trucks' sides, at the windshields. Then, one after the other, they fell to the floor as if an invisible hand had swept them clear!

Not a shot had been fired at them from the trucks—yet, in a matter of seconds, more than a dozen officers lay writhing on the cement floor, tearing at their throats—their contorted faces turning a ghastly green! Horrified, their mates stared at them. Then a weird, unreasoning panic seized upon them, drove them back. Now the way was clear, and the trucks roared away from the platform.

Vainly the Spider triggered shots after them; the mobsters were secure in the cabs, safe from his bullets....

He had failed utterly, Wentworth bitterly upbraided himself. He had been too late to save the lives of those stricken policemen. He had allowed Horeski, the man who might have led the way to the master of the Green Death, to slip through his fingers....

The blasting of shots and the nip of lead tearing at his black cape, abruptly snapped the Spider back to a realization of his own peril. The stampeded policemen had rallied. Now they were coming on again, were charging in on him... some of them reeling, toppling to the floor even as they tried to reach him!

"There he is—the Spider!" a grim-visaged lieutenant shouted furiously as he whipped up his revolver. "There's the murdering cop-killer! Get him, men! Get the—" The words died on his lips and his knees buckled beneath him.

"There he is... the Green Death...."

Wentworth caught the damning significance of the man's dying gasp as he sprang back through the doorway and started racing through the warehouse.

IT WAS hopeless to try to defend himself; those policemen would shoot him down before they listened to a word of explanation. They had no use for the Spider anyway, and this tragic episode completed his conviction in their eyes. They had *seen* their mates drop in the clutches of the Green Death, as they advanced on *him!*

In that perilous moment a possible course of action flashed into Wentworth's mind. He would have to act promptly.

Joe Horeski was a direct tie-up with the master of the Green Death and Joe Horeski was at large....

Swiftly Wentworth padded up the stairs to the dark room at the front of the building. On the floor below he could hear the police cautiously searching for him; could hear them calling warnings to one another as they advanced with guns ready. Over the glass-littered floor of the office, he picked his way to where Mack still lay huddled. The detective's heart was beating more strongly, and when Wentworth turned the flash onto his face his eyelids blinked and a moan came from his lips.

Quickly Wentworth lifted the limp form, hoisted it onto his shoulder. First of all, he must get out of that office, reach some less conspicuous spot. The police were already on the office floor, calling excitedly to one another as they came upon the wreckage. Wentworth found a side stairway that led down to the main floor and then down to the basement. There he located a long packing-case, up-ended it and stretched Mack out inside of it.

A few more minutes of unconsciousness would not hurt the wounded man—and now it was imperative that Wentworth dispose of the Spider makeup before Mack came back to his senses. Swiftly he went to work again, and when he was finished the last vestige of the ugly avenger had disappeared. It was Casimir Belotti who knelt beside Mack and examined the bullet furrow with gentle, wound-wise fingers.

As he had thought, Mack's hurt was superficial. He was opening his eyes, trying to sit up.

"Quiet!" Wentworth warned. "They are upstairs—the police

41

and some of the thieves. It is best that we remain unseen here until they are gone. Quiet, here they come!"

Mack started to protest, but he subsided when heavy footsteps came pounding down the basement stairs. With Wentworth close beside him, he lay flat in the packing case until the police, after a superficial glance around the dark basement, went back to the floor above. For long minutes the two waited there, but at last the noises upstairs subsided and they knew that the police had gone.

"You're right, Casimir," Jim Mack softly voiced the thoughts he evidently had been mulling over. "We'll handle this ourselves—you and I. The cops would only be massacred. Help me back to the lodging-house and I'll get some sleep. I'll be okay in the morning."

Cautiously Wentworth led the way upstairs and through a back window that opened onto the rear court of the building on the next street. If the police had left a guard in the warehouse, he had no intention of running afoul of it. Without interruption they made their way to the street and returned to their Bowery hideout.

Carefully he washed and dressed Mack's wound. It was not at all dangerous, but the detective had lost a lot of blood. He was weak and shaky; would be in no condition for strenuous activity in the morning—and strenuous activity was on Wentworth's next day's program. To be sure that he would not be hampered by Mack's calling the police again, he dissolved two powerful sleeping potions in water and held the glass to the detective's lips.

That should take care of Jim Mack for almost twenty-four

hours—and before that time had expired Wentworth intended to know a great deal more about the master of the Green Death....

IT WAS a little after eight o'clock the next morning when Wentworth reached the renovated East Side tenement in which Joe Horeski had his apartment. The lock on the vestibule door yielded readily to his pass-keys. But when he reached the rear of the lobby and approached the stairs he stared in amazement, an eerie chill trickling down his spine.

To one side of the stairway was a line of letterboxes with the mouth of a speaking tube above each... and hanging from one of those mouthpieces was a long green funeral crepe. Gingerly Wentworth approached the thing, pushed aside the strands of wide ribbon. Even before he read the name behind them, he knew it. Joseph Horeski... with a green crepe to signify his passing!

Wentworth's nerves were tense as he climbed the stairs and approached the gangster's door. For a few moments he listened. No sound from within, or from the other doors.

The layout of that apartment, Wentworth knew well. It ran all the way from the front of the building to the rear. In the front were Horeski's living-rooms; in the rear a large gymnasium—which, rumor had it, was also the burly thug's discipline room for any of his underlings who showed signs of rebellion. It was the gymnasium that figured largest in the plan Wentworth was about to put into execution.

From Horeski's floor he climbed three flights to the roof. Here he slipped on the overalls, cap and wide weather belt that came from a little bundle he carried under his arm. From that bundle also emerged a stout rope which he attached to a chimney, then dangled over the rear end of the roof. In the garb of a window-cleaner, he now climbed over the cornice, lowering himself until he reached Horeski's floor.

There he snapped his belt attachments to the metal rings at the sides of the window, went to work—but the rag with which he started to wipe the pane concealed a small glass-cutter... Noiselessly it described a four-inch circle just above the lock. When a wad of chewing gum was welded to the center of that cut-out circle, it took but a sharp push to punch the glass in—and the way was clear for Wentworth's hand to reach the lock.

Tensely he listened. But there was no sound in the Venetian-blind darkened room beyond. Carefully he raised the window, manipulated the blind, until he could crawl into the dark gymnasium. Still there was silence. But as he cat-footed to the front door he caught the low rumble of voices from one of the rooms beyond.

Several men were talking... and one of the voices was Horeski's! He was cursing savagely, but a note of terror, of panic, marked his ranting.

Quickly Wentworth divested himself of his window-cleaner's outfit, and again his flying fingers went to work on his face. When he was finished it was the Spider who crouched there in the gloom—the Spider come to pay a call on Joe Horeski....

One hand seized the doorknob, the other clutched an automatic. Suddenly he yanked the door wide—stared into the big living-room where Joe Horeski and three of his killers sat in chairs that faced in every direction. Their hands gripped automatics, and on the table—that was the center of their curious circle—surrounded by whiskey flasks and glasses of water, lay a tommy-gun and other weapons. Like a beleaguered garrison, their narrowed eyes watched every doorway, every window, as if expectant of attack from any side.

It was Horeski who faced the gymnasium. Convulsively his finger squeezed back on the trigger—and a stream of lead poured through the doorway. Seven shots in such rapid succession that the pistol muzzle swept upward and sent the last bullets into the ceiling... But there was no target framed in that black doorway; only darkness.

Frantically Horeski swung around to grab another weapon. But now there was an ominous figure hovering in front of him—a twisted, hunched figure with glassy eyes even more terrifying than the muzzles of his leveled automatics.

"All right, Spider—I'm licked!" the gangster gasped. "I won't hold out on you no more—I swear it! I'll give you your cut; I'll give you all we took last night...."

Suddenly his words stopped, his mouth half open. From behind him there had come a low moan, a heavy thud—and the scraping sound of a man threshing on the floor. Like an automaton, his head turned. His eyes fairly popped out of his skull as he saw one of his men writhing in a horrible death agony. A fatal green tinge was spreading over the doomed man's features. Another of the thugs staggered to his feet and pitched headlong!

"No, Spider—no!" Horeski screamed. "I know you're the

Green Death! I was a damn fool to try to gyp you. I won't no more. I—"

Suddenly his hand flashed to his throat and his words dribbled off into a slobbering groan. The fear of hell flared in his eyes as he tottered there and realized that his knees were buckling, that he was dying… great, round eyes that stared into a mirror and saw the sickening green flooding his face!

With awe almost equal to Horeski's, the Spider stared at those dying men. Four of them now, for the third of Horeski's guards toppled to the floor before his master succumbed to the murderous scourge. For once the Spider's guns were impotent; useless weights in his hands while a destroyer far more deadly than he struck witheringly out of nowhere….

Now Joe Horeski's lips were sealed. But even had he been able to talk, his revelations would have been worthless, Wentworth realized. Horeski had not known the identity of the master of the Green Death; had believed that the Spider was the grim destroyer.

The sound of Horeski's shots might bring investigators from the rest of the building, but Wentworth chanced that. Quickly he searched the room, while his fingers were swiftly removing the Spider makeup. On the top of Horeski's desk he found what he sought. Beneath a paperweight, lay a sheet of typewriter paper on which a message had been printed in green ink. This had been the gangster's death warrant.

"Only fools try to hold out on the Green Death!" it warned. "You disobeyed—and for that you will die so that other fools will know better than to follow your example. Try to escape, fool—but you are on your way to hell!" The signature was a skull-shaped smudge—of green ink.

Swift and inescapable, the Green Death had lashed out at this stupid pawn who had thought that he could profit by the terror that was sweeping the city, then refuse to pay tribute....
BUT WITH Horeski dead Wentworth was as far as ever from learning the identity of that astute super-criminal. Again he tried to locate Jigger Monahan, but the gang leader was in none of his usual haunts. Wentworth wondered whether he, too, had received one of those green-lettered warnings. The master of the Green Death was everywhere—and yet nowhere. Everywhere in the Underworld his presence was felt—yet nowhere was Wentworth able to pick up the slightest clue to his identity.

There were places where Wentworth might hope to find the leads he needed; carefully guarded rendezvous where the elite of crimedom gathered. Also there was a way in which he could penetrate those haunts, but to make the attempt would mean to put his neck in a noose....

The risk was too great, he told himself a dozen times that day. Yet before sunrise next morning he knew that he must take the chance. His conscience would no longer permit him to hesitate when an entire city trembled at the mercy of an inhuman fiend.

That night hell broke loose in Coney Island. For more than an hour the island lay helpless in the grip of an army of criminals. Fortunately, the pleasure resort's season was over and most of the amusements were closed. Nevertheless, several thousand visitors were robbed at the muzzles of tommy-guns and the tills of the concessionaires emptied.

A shrieking girl precipitated the tragedy that shocked the entire city. Her escort sprang to her rescue with his fists—then the machine-guns opened fire. What followed was appalling. Their appetites whetted by the sight of blood, the thugs went wild. Their guns turned loose in every direction. The ghastly slaughter that ensued dwarfed even the Yorkville massacre.

After that bloody night New York knew that the Underworld was in the saddle and that its demands must be met without question. Now Richard Wentworth could no longer avoid the issue. It was time for Blinky McQuade to reappear in the Underworld—Blinky McQuade, whose life was forfeit if any of his enemies discovered him.

Blinky McQuade could go where Richard Wentworth and even the Spider could not hope to penetrate. But the last time he had made his appearance, there were those criminals who had learned that he and the Spider were one. Whether or not any of them still lived, Wentworth did not know....

CHAPTER 4
DEATH COMES CALLING

FOR THE dozenth time Nita van Sloan re-read the glaring black headlines and threw down the newspaper in exasperation. "Spider Hunted For Green Death Murders!" the banner shrieked. "Arch-Criminal Identified as Cop-Killing Fiend Who Terrorizes City."

The Spider the master of the Green Death... of all the utter nonsense!

Fretfully she stared at the offending print. Gradually the rage ebbed from her violet eyes, displaced by the anxious look that comes from days and nights of constant fear. For a moment her lips quivered. Then determinedly she fought back the near panic, regained her self-control.

"Right, Dick—the chin's still up," she whispered, as if the tall, splendidly built figure she knew so well were there beside her.

It was nothing new for Nita to be sitting in the anxious seat while the man she loved hazarded his life in the endless battle for law and order—for the weak in their struggle against the ruthless encroachments of the criminally powerful. This was the price she paid for having Richard Wentworth's love, she told herself. She had no regrets over the bargain.

Beautiful, talented, she could have chosen a husband from among the wealthiest and most desirable men in the city. But the world contained only one man for her—and he was the Spider. Even though his great love for her took second place to his duty to mankind; she would not have changed him one iota, even were it within her power to do so.

For years she had known that Wentworth's doom would be sealed, were his identity as the Spider ever discovered. But then he had always had a fighting chance. Powerful friends and the security of his own social position were there to fall back upon. Now he was utterly alone, every man's hand turned against him. He had no safe home to which he might return, no loyal servants ready to aid him. Today, not only the Spider but Richard Wentworth himself was a hunted fugitive.

In the days when Police Commissioner Stanley Kirkpatrick

was in his office at headquarters this *never* could have happened. But now Kirkpatrick was a bed-ridden invalid. His place was filled by Acting Commissioner Sanford Dane—whose fondest ambition was to apprehend the Spider and prove that he and Richard Wentworth were one!

Those headlines were Sanford Dane's work; Nita knew that without being told. Two nights ago a car-load of policemen had been trapped and almost annihilated by the Green Death when they interrupted the looting of a fur warehouse. The survivors of that debacle had testified that the Spider had personally supervised the robbery; that he had invoked the Green Death to slay their comrades. Since then, the newspapers had been screaming the Spider's guilt and demanding that the police capture him.

Which was exactly what Sanford Dane wanted. Nita could visualize the short, stocky little man, with his broad shoulders and large, close-cropped head, his theatrical gestures and grandiloquent statements—could visualize him reveling in the statements he delighted in giving to the press.

"New York City today is paying the penalty for years of gross negligence," he said. "For years this super-criminal, who calls himself the Spider, was tolerated because of the supposed aid he rendered the police. Now, in his latest guise, he seeks to force the entire city to pay tribute to him on constant fear of a most horrible death.

"Fortunately, the New York Police Department, as at present constituted, does not need the services of the Spider or any other outlaw and has no fear of him. This time the brazen arch-criminal, secure in his supposed immunity to arrest and prosecution, has gone too far. He is on his way to the electric chair that should have ended his outrageous career long ago."

THAT WAS the sort of braggadocio Sanford Dane loved. Yet, behind it, Nita realized, was the shrewd, carefully calculating mind of an ambitious man. If Dane succeeded in capturing the Spider, his appointment as permanent police commissioner would be assured—and he would leave no stone unturned to attain that objective.

But, meanwhile, he had been accomplishing nothing. The wave of crime that had engulfed the city was appalling. And instead of running down the criminals responsible for it, the head of the police department was busily planning to clinch his hold on his job! Aiding and abetting him in that scheme was the district attorney, who had little use for Stanley Kirkpatrick and even less for Wentworth.

No matter what the survivors of the warehouse trap might testify, Nita of course knew that the Spider could never be guilty of such atrocious crimes. Yet, knowing him as she did, she also realized that he already had declared war on the Green Death. Therein lay his danger. For now Sanford Dane and the district attorney might manage to apprehend him, then speedily frame him. Already they had the set-up to railroad him to his doom.

Even more distressing was the fact that now she could not see Dick, could not even talk to him and know that he was well. Ever since he had been driven into hiding, the police watch on her apartment had been maintained twenty-four hours a day. Nita had provided herself with ways of leaving without being

seen. But to try to contact Wentworth might mean delivering him
into the hands of the police....

If only he would telephone... Yet
even that was dangerous, for she
knew that her phone was tapped.
Dane had a hook-up organized
by which he could send his men
racing to the other end of the line,

if Wentworth should betray his whereabouts by a call....

Nita paced the floor restlessly—then suddenly halted. Her
eyes widened as she listened to the high-pitched chatter of a
shrill buzzer. That was a call for help—a signal which was to be
used only in a case of greatest emergency! It meant that Stanley
Kirkpatrick was in grave danger!

Kirkpatrick's apartment was in the same building as Nita's,
three floors below hers. Convalescing slowly from a nervous
breakdown, his physician had prescribed absolute peace and
quiet. He received few visitors—only Nita and his personal
friends. But his helplessness had worried her considerably.
Bedridden and almost always alone, he afforded a tempting
target at which Richard Wentworth's enemies might strike.

Because of this concern Nita had won the confidence of
Marguerite, the commissioner's nurse, and had installed an
alarm between the apartments so that she could be notified if
Kirkpatrick was in danger. The concealed buzzer buttons were
located in the walls, where they could not be pressed by accident... and now that alarm was droning steadily!

Nita's nerves were tingling as she took an automatic and a key from her desk drawer, hurried downstairs. For a moment she hesitated outside Kirkpatrick's apartment door. She could barely hear the sound of a voice in the rooms beyond. Then her key was in the door, opening it noiselessly, to admit her to the foyer and living-room beyond.

Now the voice was louder—a menacing voice spitting, biting, vitriolic words that froze Nita's blood!

"—that's what you thought when you sent me to jail six years ago. You thought that I was an old fool who would forget all about you, once the prison doors closed on me. But you were sadly mistaken," the bitter voice taunted. "I promised then that I would see you when my time was up. I've come to keep my promise, Kirkpatrick. Then I was a helpless scientist who knew nothing about the law. Now I am a law unto myself—I am the one the newspapers call the Master of the Green Death!"

Nita covered the distance from the living-room to the bedroom—and stared at the astounding tableau....

MARGUERITE, HER face drained of all color, cowered, helplessly against the wall. Her round eyes glued horrifiedly on an old man who hovered beside the bed, where Kirkpatrick was propped up among pillows. In one hand the intruder held a leveled revolver; in the other a small glass of colorless liquid. But it was the oldster's face that shocked Nita even more than his gun and his threatening words. A high-boned, gaunt-cheeked face with a craggy nose and bushy gray brows; a face framed in gray hair of a length that gave him the appearance of a musician or of a poet... a dreamer rather than a man of action.

The face of a dreamer his face might once have been, but something had transformed it into the face of a devil, of a leering fiend! The eyes blazed with the fury of hell, the lips curled with acid malevolence; every line blended in molding a mask of mad hatred!

"The Master of the Green Death," he repeated the dread pseudonym with evil relish. "And now, my dear Commissioner, you are going to sample some of my excellent brew!"

The gun muzzle jabbed into Kirkpatrick's chest as the glass went toward his lips. But before the prodding barrel could force him to open his mouth, Nita sprang across the room and threw herself upon the madman. One hand seized the leveled gun, desperately thrust its muzzle away from Kirkpatrick's body. The other slapped her gun against the glass and sent it crashing to the floor—its poisonous contents dashed all over the room.

Before the raging-eyed old man could make a move against her, her weapon had him covered.

"Back against that wall—quickly!" Nita snapped at him. "Pick up his gun, Marguerite. Don't be afraid, he won't—"

A low, horrified gasp from the nurse answered her—and in the same instant she felt the cold muzzle of a pistol pressed against the back of her neck.

"Put down your gun—*please!*" a low voice gasped behind her. "Oh, don't make me kill you! I will, unless you do as I say. I—"

Nita's thoughts sped through her brain with lightning speed at that moment. The girl behind her was an amateur at this playing with guns. She was terrified—but also desperate; and that made her even more dangerous. She might pull back on

54

the trigger in sheer desperation because she could not think of anything else to do.

"All right—you win," Nita conceded, and her gun-hand lowered.

The automatic fell from her fingers. But even before it hit the floor, she had flung herself to one side, easily jerking the limited mark of her neck out of range. In the same instant she was grappling with a girl of about her own age, had hold of the pistol and was wresting it from the other's hand. But the old fellow seized his opportunity instantly. Nita saw him dart past her, reach the door just as her fingers closed on the gun barrel.

Quickly she snapped a shot after the fugitive… but the girl had leaped upon her, ruined all aim. Together they fell to the floor. The girl clung desperately, pinning Nita's arms to her sides—holding on as if she never would release her grip. Her eyes were wild with fear and low, half-strangled moans came from her clenched lips.

Then suddenly she relaxed, broke into hysterical sobbing.

The corridor was empty when Nita reached it. The self-confessed Master of the Green Death had escaped. His liberator was huddled in a crumpled heap, guarded by Marguerite's gingerly held gun, when Nita returned.

"The Master of the Green Death—we had him right here, and he got away," Kirkpatrick lamented. "If only I could have gotten out of bed—"

"He *isn't!* He *can't* be! He didn't know what he was saying!" the girl on the floor interrupted tempestuously. "Sometimes I

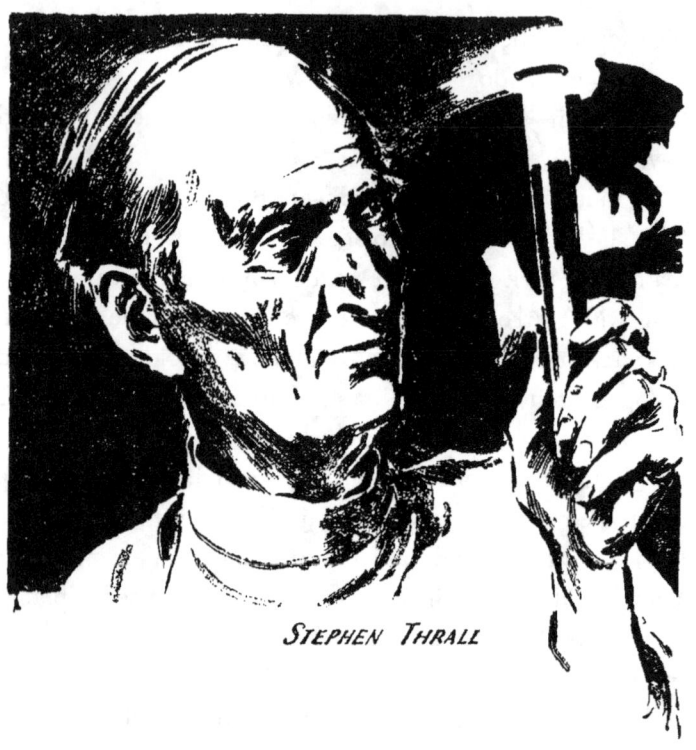

Stephen Thrall

think he may be half-mad—but he isn't bad or a murderer. He *couldn't* be that! If you knew him as I do you would understand!" **SUDDENLY SHE** turned from Kirkpatrick to Nita, her eyes brimming with tears. "You are Miss van Sloan," she identified Nita. "I knew you as soon as I saw you in the hallway—before I followed you in here.

"You are Richard Wentworth's fiancée—you must know where he is. Please tell me, Miss van Sloan—please tell me where to find him. I know that he is a fugitive himself, but he will know how to help me. I am in such terrible trouble. I don't know anyone who can help me—unless I can persuade *him!*"

"We don't know where Mr. Wentworth is ourselves," Nita told her. She helped the girl to her feet and led her to a chair. "Suppose you tell us what is troubling you. Perhaps we can advise you."

For a moment the girl looked uncertain, glanced frightenedly from Nita to Kirkpatrick. Then her hesitancy melted, and the floodgates of her confidence opened wide.

"I am Maida Thrall," she began. "My father is Professor Stephen Thrall—that was he you saw here a few minutes ago.

MAIDA THRALL

JIM MACK

You may not remember, but he was a famous brain specialist, very highly respected in the profession, until a little over six years ago. Then he got into—trouble. I never have quite understood what happened. Father was in charge of a private sanitarium, where he was doing research work, besides attending to the patients. Six of his patients, harmless brain disorder cases, turned violently insane and died in quick succession… and then the police interfered.

"You assigned detectives to the sanitarium." She turned to Kirkpatrick. "On the evidence they gathered, Father was tried and convicted of having performed illegal operations which had caused their deaths—operations to advance his own experiments. He was sentenced to nine years in prison… The parole board released him three weeks ago. He hated you bitterly when he was taken away—principally because you would not grant him a private interview and give him a chance to clear himself. He felt that he was persecuted by the police—and made some foolish threats to be avenged against you."

Kirkpatrick nodded sympathetic understanding.

"I remember—but there was nothing I could do for him," he recalled. "Once the district attorney's office had taken over the case it was out of my hands. He did not understand that."

"Prison is no place for a man like my father," Maida Thrall resumed. "It was unending torture for him. Howard Spalding—he was one of father's assistants in the sanitarium—and I visited him frequently during the six years he was confined there. We were always worried about his mental condition. We were afraid that he would suffer a complete breakdown. But when he came home he seemed to be quite normal. I was particularly glad to see that he seemed to have forgotten his hatred for Mr. Kirkpatrick and never mentioned his threats.

"But after I had been around him a few days I found that he had changed—almost imperceptibly, but changed nevertheless. I don't know just how to describe it to you. At times I fear that he is becoming a little childish. He is peculiarly secretive—won't let anyone come near him when he is working in his laboratory. He seems trying to evade me. Today I went out for a little while, and as I came home I saw him darting into a cab just in front of the house. I reached the cab just in time to hear him give your address to the driver, then he was gone.

"Something about his furtive attitude frightened me. I only took time to run inside and get that gun, and then I came here. I didn't know whom he had come to see—until I saw Mr. Kirkpatrick's name on the register. I thought I would die! You know the rest," she finished brokenly. "I can't imagine what made him come here like that. It must have been some spell that came over him. I'll watch him carefully, I promise you that. But I'm afraid... I need help so badly."

"This Howard Spalding you mentioned," Nita spoke calmly, soothingly. "He knows your father's mental condition, doesn't he? Suppose we see him and ask his advice."

Eagerly Maida Thrall grasped at that straw of hope; and half an hour later she led Nita into Spalding's bachelor apartment on East Thirty-sixth Street just off Madison Avenue.

SPALDING, A medium built, slightly bald man of about forty, met them at the door and was greatly concerned the moment he saw Maida's reddened eyes and her obvious nervous tension. Like Stephen Thrall, Spalding was a professional-looking man; but his face was rather undistinguished and commonplace—until he became excited. Then his eyes kindled and gave his whole countenance a new animation.

He was shocked when he heard what had happened—shocked and at a loss to offer an explanation.

"I am not working with the professor now," he said thoughtfully, "but I am willing to swear that he is perfectly sound mentally… and yet I cannot gainsay what you saw. It is absurd to think that he could have any connection with this terrible Green Death epidemic—perfectly absurd."

For a moment he was silent, while he pursed his lips and worked his fingers together, abstractedly.

"If only we knew what was in that glass he tried to force down the commissioner's throat," he mused. "There wasn't anything left of that potion—nothing that could be salvaged for analysis?"

"I looked for that," Nita told him. "It wasn't a very large dose—not more than two or three ounces—and that was spattered all over the thick carpet. I'm afraid there is nothing for us there."

"Perhaps I can gain his confidence," Spalding volunteered. "I'll do my best. If I can discover the contents of that glass, I'll wager I can prove the professor was bluffing beautifully. In my estimation that is the answer. He conceived some wild scheme for giving Kirkpatrick a good scare—that and nothing more."

Spalding tried to give conviction to his words, but the idea of a mature man trying to punish another by scaring him was preposterous. To Nita it only revealed how impossible it was for even his friends to supply a lucid explanation for Stephen Thrall's mad visit. To adjudge the man unbalanced was to treat him leniently—a madman whose warped brain had conceived a fiendish weapon that gave him mastery over the city's Underworld!

The threat of the Green Death that hovered over the metropolis was ghastly—and now it hung like a Damoclean sword over Stanley Kirkpatrick's helpless head; a doom that might swoop down upon him at any moment.

Something must be done to put an end to that terrible threat. But what? She must report what she had learned to the police. And be laughed at by Sanford Dane? Stanley Kirkpatrick would back her up and insist upon Stephen Thrall's arrest. How far would they get with that—except to play into Dane's hands and give him an opportunity to claim that Kirkpatrick was desperately putting up a smoke screen to cover his friend, the Spider?

For every suggestion the answer rose up to confront her immediately... and in a few moments Nita realized her utter helplessness. With Sanford Dane in command, resource to the police department was closed to her—even though she could give them a lead which might mean the end of the Green Death terror! Again the police were failing the city they were supposed to protect. Their task must devolve upon the only man who could hope to shoulder it—the Spider!

The Spider... but where was he now? How could she get in touch with him? Dick had lost himself deliberately so that she would not be able to contact him, and by so doing share his danger. But now that situation was changed. Now Stanley Kirk-patrick was in grave danger. Dick would want to know about that; would want to throw himself into the fight to protect his old friend no matter at what peril to himself.

And now she had a lead which might mean the trapping and throttling of the Master of the Green Death before additional thousands of lives were swept away in the steadily increasing tidal wave of crime. Dick would want to know that—even if he was certain that his life, and her own as well, would be sacrificed in winning the city's deliverance....

Somehow she must find him—and the only way she knew of doing that was by paying a visit to Blinky McQuade. Perhaps Wentworth was hiding out in the Holian Alley quarters—or, if not, perhaps she could leave a message there that would reach him.

Resolutely she set out for the slum abode she had never seen—the home of this other strange personality of the man she loved and all New York hunted.

CHAPTER 5
EXIT BLINKY McQUADE

THE SHABBY, grimy-windowed room that Blinky McQuade called home was located in the heart of that maze of densely populated streets that lies between the Bowery and the East River. Number One Holian Alley was his address, but Richard Wentworth approached it not by means of "Holy Alley" but by way of Pallin Place—the street which backed up against the alley and joined it to form the point of a V at Number One. In the rear of Number One Holian Alley and of Number Two Pallin Place was a small court which served both buildings as a backyard.

That desirable feature was one of the main reasons why he had chosen the alley to be Blinky McQuade's residence. It provided a double entrance and exit for both buildings—an advantage fully appreciated and utilized by their tenants.

Slipping in through the Pallin Place entrance, Wentworth eyed the courtyard cautiously and crossed it to the door of his own tenement. Up the rickety stairs to the second floor he climbed. There he opened the door of a rear room that was nearly bare of furnishings other than a huge bed which filled most of it. In the center of this he kneeled, to manipulate a spring which released part of the massive headboard and opened it out into a fully equipped makeup table.

In a few minutes the gaunt cheeks, deep-set eyes and indescribably foreign appearance of Casimir Belotti began to fade—and into their place came the frowsy countenance of Blinky McQuade. Skillfully Wentworth applied skin lotions, mouth pads, hair grease. When he was finished, he had become a loose-lipped, disheveled-looking individual who peered out at the world through thick-lensed, metal-hooded glasses. With the addition of a grimy, frayed collared shirt and a wrinkled, grease-stained suit, Blinky McQuade was complete—ready to shuffle downstairs into the crowded, noisy street, a surly, grumbling derelict of a man who blended perfectly with the sidewalk throngs that jostled him as he passed.

Nobody in those busy streets seemed to pay the slightest attention to him, but Wentworth's nerves were tense, his keen eyes sharp behind their screening spectacles. He knew the deception of this apparent indifference; knew that he was being scrutinized from many points as he went from block to block... realized that death would follow close behind him if any of those searching glances revealed his true identity.

The Master of the Green Death had set his mark on this seething cauldron of humanity. Wentworth recognized it in many ways—but none more forcefully than when he saw that the police were patrolling their beats in pairs! Strapping bluecoats who had lost all their easy camaraderie of other days. Now they were tense, watchful, ready for trouble at any minute; like men who patrol the edge of a volcano that is expected to erupt at any moment. Men who had the shadow of haunting fear deep in their eyes... A small Italian grocery store was the first place Blinky McQuade visited. Its single show window was piled high with tins of olive oil, hung with ancient-looking bolognas. Inside, the shelves were lined with the same merchandise, augmented by bins of spaghetti and macaroni.

"Hi, Dominic," Blinky greeted, when a portly, gray-haired old man with a spectacular mustache nodded to him from behind the counter. "Pint of the usual—and I hope to tell it's better than last time."

Dominic Santacrocci grinned amiably and disappeared through the curtain at his back. When he returned he palmed an unlabeled pint flask that was filled with a reddish liquid.

"Sixty cent," he proclaimed—and cautiously held back the bottle of bootleg for payment.

"Sixty cents!" Blinky exploded. "Cripes! How d'you get that way? Fifty's all you ever got for that rot-gut—an' then you were gettin' double pay. Sixty cents!"

"It is the tax." Santacrocci shrugged his shoulders and held out the palms of his hands in a gesture of helplessness. "You been away, Mr. Blink—that's right, no? Everybody know about the tax."

"What tax?" Blinky snarled suspiciously. "I ain't read about the gov'ment passin' no new taxes."

"Not the gover'ment, Mr. Blink," old Dominic soothed. "The gover'ment taxes"—he grinned—"they easy… but not this one. This different. Everybody he pay this tax or—*poof!*—too bad for him. I pay, but I make more money. Everybody he have money now…."

And old Dominic was started. Before he was finished Wentworth had pumped the garrulous old bootlegger dry. Now he began to understand the extent of the grip the wielder of the Green Death had fastened on this poorest section of the city. Every storekeeper, in those shop-lined slum streets was paying the "tax"; was yielding ten percent of his sales to the collectors—and was not complaining because of the increase of bootleg business.

Times were good in this ordinarily poverty-ridden district. Men were making money. How? Dominic winked—and turned to wait on another customer who, in former days, had never had the price to buy even a single glass of the cheapest bar whiskey.…

From Santacrocci's, Blinky McQuade went on to nearly a dozen other places—to bars and pool rooms, coffee pots and "social clubs," barber shops and the cheapest of flop-houses— the highest and lowest of the Underworld's multitudinous

"There's another way out of here,
Gallagher—open it up fast!"

establishments. In each he nodded to acquaintances, bought drinks or loafed idly while he gossiped or listened to the hum of voices around him. In all of them he quickly sensed the great change that had taken place. And he had been lucky enough not to be recognized by any of his enemies....

HE DISCOVERED that the Underworld had lost all fear of the police. Now when thieves and hold-up men went out to do a job it was with the certainty that they would not be apprehended. The ever-present Green Death would mysteriously strike down anyone who attempted to interfere with them. All that was necessary was that they hand over ten percent of their take—the master's tithe.

"But how d'you get it up?" Blinky questioned one man. "Where d'you go with it? Nobody seems to know who in hell this Green Death is or where to find him."

"Don't have to know," the half-intoxicated pickpocket grinned owlishly. "No business of ours who he is. Hell with that. He takes care o' things and tells us where to ante up. That's all we gotta know."

Out of his pocket he took a folded tabloid and opened it to the personal column; ran his finger down the items until he came to one that he pointed out triumphantly. Wentworth read, "Joe: National wishes visit before two. Gordon Downs." Twice he re-read that meaningless line, then turned sneeringly to the smirking thief.

"Sure, great stuff—just like a lot o' Greek," he growled. "What in hell's it s'posed to mean?"

"Easy," came the chuckling explanation. "You see that

'Gordon Downs,' don't you? Never happened to think that those initials might stand for 'Green Death,' did you? Well, let's say they did—then we'd start at the beginning and count the letters in the words. Three for Joe, eight for national—put 'em together and they might just happen to mean Thirty-eighth Street, huh? Same way with the next two; they might happen to be number sixty-five—right? 'Before two'—that's the time you better have it on the line, boy, or you're gonna be outta luck."

A warning scowl from the bartender clamped the pickpocket's mouth shut—but Wentworth had the secret of the ingenious collection system. Not a very devious cipher to unravel—and Wentworth had a shrewd hunch that the Green Death did not particularly care whether or not it was solved by other than those for whom it was intended. His brazen use of the daily papers to give his orders was indicative of the man's sheer contempt for the law, his confidence in his own deadly power....

More and more Wentworth began to respect the evil genius against whom he had pitted himself. A catastrophic fate hung over New York City. Given a few more weeks, the master of the Green Death would be supreme in the metropolis, a ruthless overlord who would wring every possible dollar from the helpless citizens... and then what? Then would come chaos, an unchecked, city-wide riot to eclipse anything the world had ever seen!

Wentworth's blood chilled at the prospect of the Underworld, no longer bought off with the easy tribute to which they had become accustomed, turning like a pack of wolves on the helpless, pauperized population. That was what New York faced, unless he could come to grips with this diabolical criminal fiend....

Place after place Wentworth visited, but it was not until late in the afternoon that he met Deuce Behrman in Gallagher's "stop-over joint" and uncovered a lead that brought him up like a fox-hound on a fresh scent.

Gallagher's was one of the most exclusive haunts of the Underworld's elite; a place where a police record was a prerequisite for admission. Situated in a rear house that could only be reached after passing a watchful guard, who was stationed in the hallway of the street-front building, the place served as a hotel for those who found it expedient to disappear from the city for a few days or a few weeks. Gallagher's prices were high—but he asked no questions of his guests, and he guaranteed them against the embarrassment of unexpected police visits.

IT WAS dusk when Blinky shuffled into the narrow, garlic-smelling hallway of the outer building and pressed his hands against both sides of the doorway at its rear. With that pressure, a panel in the upper part of the door raised several inches so that he might be inspected by a pair of cold eyes from the cubbyhole beyond. The guard satisfied, the door was opened, and Blinky passed through a ten-foot vestibule, through another doorway and into the twenty-five foot courtyard that separated the front building from Gallagher's.

Gallagher's bar was seldom crowded, but today there were more men lined up in it than Wentworth had ever seen there. A dozen pairs of eyes turned in his direction as he entered, and there were still others sitting in the booths and gathered around a poker table at the rear. Half of them Wentworth knew by sight—but at the far end of the bar he spied one who was more than a casual acquaintance.

Deuce Behrman, despite his pretensions and his too-flashy clothes, was only a petty gangster, his sobriquet indicative of the esteem in which the Underworld held him. About a year before, he had been one of scores of unimportant pawns utilized by a criminal whom the Spider was out to smash; and in the clean-up Blinky McQuade had saved him from certain death. Behrman affected to have forgotten all about that—but Wentworth knew that, in his own way, the fellow was grateful.

Now he looked up with barely a nod of recognition as Blinky shuffled up to his end of the bar. But after they had downed two whiskies together he forgot his pose and became friendly.

"You got back to town just in time, Blinky," he confided. "Things are popping here—and I'm in the know."

"What kinda racket?" Blinky demanded suspiciously. "I'm takin' things easy for a while, and I ain't aimin' to spend my vacation up-river."

"Nothing to worry about—not a thing," Behrman assured him quickly. "This is the safest thing you ever tackled. The Green Death—you heard of him? He's covering us—and that's all we need. We got the cops just where we want them. I been in three jobs already—and not a cop could lay a hand on us. Tomorrow night we pull the biggest thing that's happened in this town in years. You're a sap if you don't come in on it."

Blinky McQuade seemed far from impressed, but now Behrman leaned forward and argued with missionary zeal.

"Listen, Blinky," he urged. "We been guaranteed at least a grand a piece for less than half an hour's work. All you gotta do...."

Even as he listened to Behrman's low voice, Wentworth sensed a change in the barroom—a peculiar, ominous hush that had settled over it. His nerves tensed and the hairs at the nape of his neck felt as if they were beginning to rise—when a hoarse, snarling voice knifed through the sudden stillness.

"Hello, Spider!" a scarred-faced thug who had just risen from the card table flung across the bar. "Yeah, I know who you are, McQuade—I'm one gent you didn't kill off with your dirty double-crossing!" Now his voice had risen and he turned to face the rest of the room. "That's the Spider—the rat who killed Healey and Wolufski and Deegan!" he shouted. "He's in here now to get the rest of you! Get him before—"

For an infinitesimal part of a second there was silence in that stunned bar. Men's eyes opened wide and their hands seemed frozen wherever they happened to be. They hated the Spider and would not hesitate to shoot him down. But now they knew he was right there beside them, a strength-sapping fear gripped them and held them immobile.

Only Behrman seemed capable of movement. The color drained from his face and left it an ashen gray. But he managed to control his muscles to force himself slowly back away from that presence that had suddenly become far more deadly than the worst plague. And he was just in time—for he had barely edged away from Blinky when the impending storm suddenly broke.

"Not in here! Not in my place!" Gallagher yelled frantically. But his voice was drowned by a deafening roar of shots.

FROM A dozen points in that room flame spurted at Blinky McQuade's end of the bar—but the bullets smashed into the bar mirror and drilled into the walls. A split-second before that fusillade, Blinky had flung himself to one side—then leaped straight at his accuser. Twin automatics flashed into his hands. Even as he sprang, his bullets were hammering into the lights, winking them out one after the other—until the only illumination came from the dimly lighted back-bar closets.

"Get him, the dirty rat!" the scar-faced thug screamed desperately. His panic-stricken warning died on his lips as one of Blinky's guns crashed down on his skull.

Then Blinky was past him, had reached the card table. The players were springing to their feet, ducking for cover. Like a darting rabbit, he dived beneath the table—came up with it on his back. He grasped it by the legs and used it as a huge shield as he charged the length of the bar—wiping it clear of his enemies.

Before the thugs could concentrate their fire upon it, he hurled the table straight into their midst. Howls and yells of agony came from every part of the room, keening above the guns. Now the place had become a weirdly illuminated inferno. Shots were blazing from every corner, bottles and mirrors smashing, chairs overturning and splintering underfoot, men leaping and tumbling over one another. Blinky McQuade was safe on the floor, close to the bar rail. Steadily he edged his way along—not toward the doors, which were steel-plated and had been securely locked from behind the bar at the first sign of trouble, but toward the spot where Gallagher was bellowing demands that the fighting cease.

Suddenly Blinky jabbed a gun into his ribs, fastened a hand in the proprietor's collar.

"There's another way out of here, Gallagher," he clipped. "Open it up—fast! You heard what that mug said—I am the Spider!"

Gallagher's fat body was shaking. He tried to speak, but the words stuck in his throat. The gun muzzle jabbed deeper, and he sagged like a deflated balloon. For an instant Wentworth feared the man would collapse. Then Gallagher docilely led the way through a gateway that swung open in the side of the bar.

A barrage of bottles from the terrified bartender greeted them, but a roar of Wentworth's gun flung the man flat on the floor. Like an automaton Gallagher crawled forward, hooked his fingers in the duckboards. He lifted—and a hinged trapdoor swung up. Wentworth was close at his back as he led the way down a ladder into a dark, narrow tunnel.

"If you're thinking of trying anything—don't, Gallagher," Wentworth warned.

"God—not me, Spider!" the other quavered. "I didn't have nothing to do with this!"

He led the way up another ladder and through a trapdoor that opened into a furnished room. Wentworth had gauged the distance he had come through the tunnel and now noted the position of the door. He was fairly certain that he was in one of the rear rooms of the building in front of Gallagher's.

He inched the door open, saw that he was correct. That door

was about ten feet in front of the rear-of-the-hall door that led to Gallagher's—the door behind which the guard was stationed.

"Okay, Gallagher—you first," Wentworth ordered. He almost had to lift the trembling proprietor out into the hall.

As soon as Wentworth stepped over the threshold, he whirled Gallagher. Now the man's body was between him and the rear door. A stream of blasting lead poured from the suddenly opened panel. Frantically Gallagher screamed an order not to fire, but was too late... the trap set for the Spider had snared himself. Bullets tore into him and he pitched to the floor. Wentworth snapped a shot over his falling body—stabbing a black hole between the vestibule guardian's cold eyes.

BLINKY McQUADE was out in the street, mingling with the passers-by, before the sound of the shots had gathered a crowd. But now he knew that there was no time to lose. He must get back to Holian Alley, change into Casimir Belotti's outfit. Blinky McQuade had been under suspicion before; now his usefulness was ended. Within half an hour he would be a marked character, hunted high and low, target for every gangster gun....

As he approached his Holian Alley hideaway, caution prompted him to enter by way of the Pallin Place building. The moment he reached the triangular courtyard, he gave silent thanks for that saving forethought. From the Pallin Place doorway he eyed the windows of his room—and caught a fleeting reflection in one of them. Just a narrow, perpendicular streak of light that blinked out immediately. It told him that his room was being watched from the one across the court that almost joined it at the base of the courtyard's V!

That room, so close to his own, was occupied by a young girl who had done him favors on several occasions. Once he had used her quarters as a hurried means of egress from his own. Again, she had flown a signal from her window to warn him that danger waited behind his own door. Curiously tonight nothing indicated an ambush.

Wentworth edged his way along the wall of the building until he could cross the courtyard and look up at it from the wall of its Holian Alley neighbor. The room across from his own was dark, although he was certain there had been a light in it a few moments before. For several minutes nothing happened. Then he saw the drawn shade at the girl's window being surreptitiously edged to one side for a few seconds—long enough for keen eyes to scrutinize his windows. Again it fell back into place. Now Wentworth's suspicions were fully aroused.

Quickly he retraced his steps to the Pallin Place doorway, padded softly up the steps to the second floor. Not a sound came from the girl's room when he stood outside her door… but he was certain that someone was inside.

From his pocket he took a small ring of skeleton keys, selecting one to pick the simple lock. With infinite care he inserted it, applied a slight pressure. The lock began to turn. Gripping the key firmly so as not to let the mechanism of the lock click over loudly, he turned it with no more speed than the second hand of a watch. The revolution was completed without a sound. He fastened his fingers over the doorknob, turned it noiselessly.

Now he caught the first sound from within. The creak of a board, the soft tread of footsteps—the barely audible sound of the shade being pulled aside. The room would be dark, but Wentworth had taken the precaution to put out the hall light as he passed it. Cautiously he started to inch the door open; had it barely started when his fingers froze on the knob.

That was a groan from inside! A groan—and then the sound of a body threshing and tossing on a squeaky-springed bed!

Wentworth tensed, ready to leap through the doorway and close with whoever might be beyond it. When once more amazement held him spellbound.

"Take it easy, sister; nobody's going to hurt you," a man's voice was saying. "Maybe you're not so comfortable there. But if you'd been willing to listen to reason I wouldn't have tied you up."

That voice was unmistakable—the voice of Jim Mack, the detective! Jim Mack, doggedly trailing the Spider—and getting warmer by the minute! So Mack, too, probably had learned that Blinky McQuade and the Spider were the same person....

Wentworth's thoughts came lightning-fast. He did not want to harm Mack. But the detective must be dislodged from that room—speedily if Wentworth was to get across to his own room before the gang avengers were upon him.

Carefully drawing the door closed again, Wentworth tiptoed back to the head of the stairs. Then he returned at a normal walk, to knock boldly on Catherine O'Keefe's door. Not a sound answered him—except the barely audible creaking of the bed. Wentworth reached into his pocket and brought out the ring of keys, rattled them ostentatiously—then thrust one into the keyhole.

That brought quick results. He could hear Mack cat footing

across the floor, could hear him come to a stop just beyond the doorway. Then Wentworth flung the door wide, leaped inside. Knocked off his feet by the swinging door, Mack thumped to the floor. Before he could regain his feet, Wentworth caught him on the point of the jaw with a swift, merciful uppercut. Again Jim Mack crashed to the floor. This time he stayed down....

Assured that the detective would not arise again, Wentworth turned on the light, closed the door. One glance told him that Mack would not revive for some time. By then he would be securely bound and gagged. Wentworth bent over the bed, took the gag from between the O'Keefe girl's jaws. He started to untie her hands.

"Thanks, Blinky," she said simply. "You handled that swell. Better watch yourself, though—he's a cop. He came in here a little while ago and tried to get me to let him watch your place from my window—"

"I know," Blinky cut her short. "I been expecting something like this. The heat's on for me. Gotta scram for a while. I'll tie him up with these ropes he put on you and leave him here till I'm ready to skip. Watch over him till I come back, like a good kid—will you?"

Catherine O'Keefe helped him tie up the unconscious detective so that he need lose no time. Then Wentworth left her and hurried across the court to his own room. Quickly he changed back into Casimir Belotti's clothes. Then, kneeling in front of the bedstead make-up table, he began to obliterate the frowsy face of Blinky McQuade—the face that never again must be resurrected....

He had hardly begun to cream his face when there was a knock on the door. He tensed, stayed absolutely quiet, made no answer. The knock was repeated. This time it was in a code that he could not mistake. That was Nita's knock! She was outside there in the tenement hallway!

Instinctively he turned toward the door, then stopped. She must stay there. He couldn't let her embroil herself in the deadly peril that threatened him….

But Nita van Sloan's hearing was as keen as his own. "Please let me in, Dick," she pleaded softly, her lips close to the door panel. "I know you are in there; I heard you. I wouldn't have come, but I must see you. This is important."

Wentworth had resolutely deafened his ears to her pleas—but suddenly he caught the shrill of police whistles! Instantly he knew what had happened. Nita had been followed from her apartment and trailed to Holian Alley. Now the police were closing in on the building; they would trap her out there in the hall!

QUICKLY HE stepped to the door, let her in. The hallway was still empty, but he heard more whistles shrilling out on the street, men shouting directions. It would be only a matter of minutes or less before they were up there battering down his door. Grimly he closed and locked it, turned back into the room—and stopped again, to stare at Nita in consternation. Then with a bound he was past her; was beside one of his raggedly curtained windows. Drawing the grease-stained shade aside, he peered out into the courtyard.

His ears had not deceived him. Half a dozen shadowy figures

were down there in the little enclosure, more coming through the Pallin Place doorway. The gangster killers had come for *him!* Now he and Nita were surrounded, hemmed in from the back and from the front by enemies!

"I'm sorry, Dick," Nita whispered. "I don't see how the police could have followed me. It was so urgent that I see you—"

"Don't worry about it, darling," Wentworth said. For a minute she clung to him. Then he flung himself on his knees in front of the make-up table, went to work on his face. "Perhaps you have brought the answer to my problem."

His brain was churning at top speed. The police coming in from Holian Alley... The gangsters swarming in from Pallin Place... It was just possible that he might be able to work it, but it must be done fast.

"What happened, dear?" he asked, as his flying fingers completed the transformation and brought Casimir Belotti back into being. "Tell me quickly."

Succinctly Nita sketched what had happened in Kirkpatrick's apartment, and her subsequent visit to Howard Spalding.

"The Green Death!" he said, musingly. "The old man sounds more like a lunatic than anything else. I remember the case now—remember it very well."

"Thrall probably is mad," Nita agreed. "How much truth there may be to his claim is problematical, but there is no doubt that he broke in on Stanley with murderous intent. If I had not arrived when I did—"

That was as far as she got. Now the police were downstairs in the hallway. Wentworth heard them starting up the stairs. It was time to put his swiftly formed plan into execution. Pushing Nita back out of range, he stepped to one of the windows. As if by accident, he released one of the shades and let it snap up on its roller-standing in full view, momentarily, at the curtains.

"There he is!" a voice yelled from the courtyard.

Instantly shots barked. Bullets drilled at the window, shattered the glass, whined into the room. The whole court was in turmoil. Windows were thrown up; faces appeared on every side. From behind the curtain Wentworth triggered two quick shots down into the gangsters, then ran heavily across the floor to his door—and his stratagem worked!

"He's getting away!" someone shouted excitedly. "Stop him!"

With a rush they swarmed through the Holian Alley doorway—right into the arms of the police. The officers, held downstairs by the sound of firing from Blinky's room, were alert and waiting. To them, the on-rushing gangsters seemed allies of Wentworth's come to snatch him. They were fully prepared for such an attempt.

"The cops!" one of the gangsters howled a warning; but immediately his shout was echoed by another. "To hell with the cops! They can't do nothin'!"

It loosed pandemonium. The hallway reverberated with the thunder of shots and the savage curses of struggling men. Twice the gangsters charged into the police. But this time, curiously, the bluecoats did not drop, stricken by the Green Death. They met the killers with nightsticks and blackjacks, traded shot for shot and drove them back into the courtyard.

In the midst of the mêlée Wentworth opened his door and

stole to the head of the stairs. The hallway below was solidly packed with struggling men. All hope of escape in that direction was gone. The courtyard was just as bad. Only one possible exit remained.

He turned out his light, raised the frame of the shattered window. The gangsters below were now too busily engaged to watch what he was doing—but Catherine O'Keefe's sharp eyes were missing nothing. She saw him the moment he appeared at the window—and understood his purpose. Quickly she raised her own window and drew back the curtains, leaned out to take Nita's hand and help her step across the gap.

Nita crossed without being seen, but when Wentworth stepped up on the windowsill a shout went up from below. Shots blazed out at him and bullets flattened against the bricks within an inch of his head. He swung across the aperture. Like a pack of wolves on a fresh scent, the gangsters dived toward the Pallin Place doorway—only to be met by a fresh burst of shots from the police, now closing in on the court from both buildings.

That was exactly what Wentworth wanted. It solved the disposition of Jim Mack, and still left open the way of escape.

Quickly he lifted the detective's unconscious body, swung it over his shoulder, carried him out into the hallway and up one flight of stairs. There he propped Mack up against the wall, where the police would be sure to find him. They were already coming up the stairs, pounding on Catherine O'Keefe's door.

Before she opened, Wentworth and Nita had reached the roof—a floor higher than the Holian Alley building. They made their way up Pallin Place through a maze of chimneys, radio aerials and roof kiosks. Six houses removed from the one they had entered, they pried open a kiosk and hurried down the stairs to the basement. A cellar door admitted them to the backyard, separated by only an easily scaled fence from a court behind one of the buildings on Belmer Street—which formed the third side of the block's V-triangle.

WHEN WENTWORTH led the way out onto Belmer Street, the whole neighborhood was blaring with the wail of sirens and shriek of police whistles. Bluecoats swarmed everywhere, driving back the curious crowd that jammed the streets. As they threw a cordon around the entire block the very man they sought was unknowingly pushed back with the rest. A few minutes later Wentworth and Nita were in a taxicab on their way across town.

Blinky McQuade's career was finished, and the Holian Alley hideout must now be a thing of the past. Wentworth did not dare resume his residence in the rooming-house where he had met Jim Mack. A return to the Bowery lodging-house was equally undesirable—for there he would be found by Jim Mack. There was work to be done which the Spider could better handle alone.

That meant a new hideout. One promptly popped into his mind—a cheap hotel on Chambers Street, where he could get a top-floor room with dormer windows that opened onto a sea of rooftops. The place was filled with peddlers and beggars, ideal company for Casimir Belotti.

"I want you to get back uptown quickly," he planned swiftly, as Nita held one of his hands between both of hers. "Kirk can't be left alone in his apartment. Have Jackson or Ram Singh stay with him, and if anything happens get word to me immediately. I shall be at the Metropolitan Hotel, on Chambers Street. There are no phones in the rooms, but the clerk will take a message."

"I know," Nita said softly. "That terrible place! To think of you staying there! Sometimes I wonder how long we must go on like this... It has never been so hard on you. Dick, can't we chuck it all? We have money enough, we can get out of New York. We can go somewhere else where you will be safe. We still have a chance to do that, Dick—but our chance is slipping. Soon it really may be too late!"

Her shoulders were shaking as Wentworth's arms went around her; her voice was trembling, close to breaking. By those signs, so unusual for Nita, he knew what she was enduring—what this enforced separation and worry was costing her. His heart ached, but his duty was stern and uncompromising.

"We can't run out on Kirk—you wouldn't let me do that," he reminded her gently. "He needs us both now—and this city needs us, too. This Green Death must be ended, and then—"

The pressure of her lips silenced him. For a long moment they clung together. Then Nita released him.

"Take care of yourself, Dick," she whispered, when the cab slowed to a stop and he stepped out. "You are right. You're always right. We *must* go on. It was just that I have been so afraid... for you."

As Wentworth turned away, he heard a newsboy's shout.

"Wuxtra! Wuxtra! Pennsylvania Station dynamited!

Hundreds of Long Island commuters killed! Fifty cops dead! Read all about it! Read all about the Green Death!"

Yes, God knew that his duty lay here....

CHAPTER 6
DEATH'S PAY-DAY RAIDERS

WENTWORTH HAD told Nita that he remembered the Thrall case, and now the details came back sharply. He recalled a discussion he had had with Kirkpatrick over the threats that seemed so strange—coming from a man of the professor's caliber. Oddly, Thrall's hatred had centered not upon Franklin Penney, the assistant district attorney who convicted him—but entirely upon the police commissioner. Yet Kirk had done no more than assign the detectives who obtained the evidence Penney had utilized in court.

Thrall seemed to have forgotten all about Penney, who was now a prominent and notorious criminals' attorney. But his hatred against Kirkpatrick had not cooled even with the passing of years. It had unbalanced his once fine mind....

The professor would bear investigation, but something more important and immediate demanded Wentworth's attention. Tomorrow, according to Deuce Behrman, the Green Death intended to stage the most spectacular crime in this entire reign of lawlessness.

What was the exact nature of the scheme? If his exposure as the Spider had not precipitated the riot in Gallagher's, Wentworth might have secured the details. But that unfortunate iden-

NITA VAN SLOAN •

tification had done more than merely render Blinky McQuade's role useless. It had effectively sealed Behrman's lips. Even if Wentworth dared try the McQuade role again, the petty gangster would not talk.

No, Behrman would not talk to Blinky McQuade... But there still remained the Spider!

Wentworth remembered the gangster's ashen face, abject terror. His own decision was made. He knew the East Side walk-up where Behrman kept a flat; and twenty minutes later he stood outside the building, peering up at the dark windows. No sound came from Behrman's rooms, when he went upstairs and listened at the door. There was no response when he returned to the vestibule and pressed the bell.

This was all he wanted to know. Going upstairs again, Wentworth fell back on his skeleton keys. He stepped into the gaudily furnished living-room that was Behrman's pride. The flat was empty; Behrman had not yet come home for the night. Wentworth set about preparing a suitable reception for him.

Using the gangster's bathroom mirror, he went to work with make-up kit. Swiftly his flying fingers recreated the fearsomely ugly countenance of the Spider. The ebon habiliments went in place over his head and shoulders. Now he was ready for an interview with Deuce Behrman. In the gangster's living room he settled himself in a big armchair that commanded the doorway, started his vigil.

For hours he sat there, his mind busily engaged with the problem of the Green Death... It was early morning when at last footsteps came down the hallway and stopped at Behrman's door. A key turned in the lock, the door opened, the gangster stepped inside and fumbled for the light. Then Deuce Behrman almost fainted!

White-faced, eyes as round as saucers, mouth gaping open ludicrously, he flattened himself against the wall. For a terrifying apparition gazed at him from his favorite chair. Leveled automatics covered him. All that his mind could register was that ghastly face of the Spider!

Behrman made two ineffectual attempts to speak, but his tongue was glued to the dry roof of his mouth. Cold sweat beaded on his brow; his legs seemed to be folded under him.

"Sit down, Behrman." The Spider's rasping words were like the lash of a whip.

Somehow Behrman found a chair, dropped limply into it. He wondered as he did so whether he ever would rise again. Would those pistols perforate him as he sat there and leave him slumped in the chair with a crimson spider stamped on his forehead? He could almost feel the brand burning deeply into his skull....

"Talk, Behrman," the rasping voice commanded. "Talk fast. What is this deviltry that is scheduled for tomorrow night?"

"I—I don't know, Spider! So help me God, I don't know!" the perspiration-soaked gangster blurted. "All I know is it's going to be something big. A holdup, I think—but I'm not sure. They told us there wouldn't be any danger and we'd each get a grand out of it—maybe more."

It was just as Wentworth feared. Deuce Behrman was only an insignificant pawn in the Green Death's game. Yet, sometimes, even a pawn might checkmate a king....

Behrman's contact with the Green Death, Wentworth learned, was through Blackie Leahy, one of Jigger Monahan's lieutenants. It was Leahy who had promised him the thousand dollars and ordered him to report at four o'clock the next afternoon. Wentworth made a note of the address of the rendezvous, then announced his own program.

"I am staying here with you until three-thirty tomorrow afternoon," he decreed. "Then I am going to put on your clothes and take your place. Get undressed—you're going to bed."

Behrman tried to protest, but the snarl on that ugly face stilled him. Meekly he undressed, got into bed. The Spider lashed his wrists and ankles tying him securely to the bedstead. It seemed impossible that he would be able to sleep that night, but finally his terror-frayed nerves quieted. When he awoke it was to find a double of himself standing over him!

"Sorry to put you to this inconvenience, brother," the masquerader said, "but I have to play safe. Open up the mouth." Even the voice was a ringer for his own.

Behrman obeyed, and a gag was thrust between his jaws, tightly bound there. It would take him hours to chew through and yell for help. For a moment the man who now looked so much like himself stood preening himself in front of a mirror in typical Behrman style. Then the quailing gangster sighed relievedly. The door of the flat had closed—and the Spider was gone....

FROM BEHRMAN'S flat Wentworth took a leisurely course toward the address the gangster had given him. Blackie Leahy's rendezvous was in an empty factory building near the East River. Wentworth wanted to arrive late enough to avoid as many dangerous contacts as possible. On the way, he stopped at two bars where Behrman was well known. In each he was greeted hospitably. His make-up had passed muster. The only stumbling block might be information which Behrman was expected to possess.

It was nearly four-thirty when he arrived at the big brick building and went around to the side door. A score of cars were parked in the factory yard, and Wentworth realized the bragging gangster had not exaggerated the magnitude of this gathering.

Squaring his shoulders and affecting Deuce's self-important swagger, he pushed open the door and stepped into a partitioned-off hallway. Here a little, rat-faced gunman paced up and down restlessly. The moment the door opened, the fellow whirled. Then he glanced at his wristwatch significantly.

"Late again, eh?" Wentworth laughed. "Trouble with me is I'm too confounded popular these days. Keeps a feller busy."

"Save that for Blackie, if he's interested," the door guard growled. "What I wanta know is where is my deck? Come across; don't stand there. You know damn well I'm all out."

He held out his hand expectantly—and Wentworth cast about frantically for the key to this situation. The gunman's vicious face was twisting into a snarl; his little, pinpoint eyes were becoming venomous. Pinpoint eyes—that was it! He was a dope-fiend, a coke addict; and he expected Deuce Behrman to bring him a fresh "deck" of the white powders. So Behrman was a dope-peddler along with his various other activities....

"Geez—I've got to let you down," Wentworth said quickly. "I did my best—the stuff just didn't come through. Hell, I can't *make* it, not even for you."

"You kiddin' me?" The gunman came forward like a stalking puma, and Wentworth's nerves tensed, certain that now his masquerade must be discovered. But the killer came no closer. "By God, you're not!" he swore bitterly. "Get inside there before I let you have it!"

Wentworth needed no urging. He slipped through the doorway, hurrying down a corridor to a huge loft that was still furnished with the long benches at which leather goods workers, who were employed there, had once sat. Now the room was filled with as choice an assortment of cutthroats as he had ever seen. Fully a hundred sat on the tables or stood around in little groups. Six, who seemed to be their leaders, stood talking at a central table with Leahy.

Wentworth waited.

Another new arrival drifted in after Wentworth. Then Leahy called them to order.

"All right," he raised his voice so that the hum of conversation stopped and every eye turned his way. "Now that even Honti and Behrman are here, maybe we can get started. We've got to work on schedule today. No getting goin' whenever we feel like it; we're part of a big-time hold-up that's gonna stand this town right on its ear. Just part of it, like I said. There's a dozen other outfits like this getting together in other parts of the city—maybe more, for all I know.

"That's why we've kept this thing under our hats—so there wouldn't be any leak. The job's too big to have any mug with a loose jaw queer it. Today's Friday, you know that. Friday is payday for most of the workers in this town. So what does that mean?

It means that the subway is gonna be loaded down with jack during the rush hour. The cars will be jammed. Men and women will be carrying pay envelopes—not to mention rings and watches that'll be worth taking.

"Yeah, you got it." He grinned widely. "We're sticking up the subway in regular old Wild West style! The lay is this. Our job is the Brooklyn Bridge station of the East Side sub. Other gangs are handling Fourteenth, Times Square, Grand Central—all the big stops where the crowds is thick. We divide up into eight crews before we go to the station. We go down on the platforms—four crews on the uptown and four on the downtown. Two of the

The plunged into the darkness
between the tracks, as the Spider's
guns began working!

92

uptown crews take the first express and the first local that comes along. The other two wait and take the second. The same way with the downtown crews—they take care of two locals and two expresses. That plain?

"Okay. The train pulls out of the station and we let it get half-way to the next one. Then the motorman feels a gun jabbing him in the ribs and puts on the brakes. One man stays there to keep him covered. The rest of the crew is split in half. One half in front of the first car and the other in the rear of the last. When the train stops, they go to work—two men with sacks to make the collection and four with gats in both fists to see that nobody squawks.

"I mean that about stopping the squawks," he repeated. "You fellers who do the gun-work—don't be afraid to cut loose. If anyone starts trouble, let 'em have it. Let 'em see from the start that you mean business and they'll fold up like a lot of lambs. There ain't nothing to be afraid of. The passengers won't dare make a move against a gun, and the cops are all taken care of. The Green Death is tending to that—you're covered complete."

The Green Death! The very mention of that dread name acted like a tonic. Every sign of doubt vanished from those wolfish faces the moment they heard it. The Green Death would take care of them, would countenance any hellish barbarity they chose to perpetrate. They licked their lips at the prospect!

"We got twenty minutes to get going," Blackie Leahy finished. "Up here we've got the lists—got everybody assigned to his job. All you have to do is find out what crew you go with and what part of the job you're supposed to handle."

THE CORPSE BROKER

A DARING subway hold-up that would paralyze traffic at the height of the rush hour! Wentworth was staggered by the enormity of the horror that would happen when those devilish crews went to work. Thousands of passengers packed helplessly in the cars, unable to escape, unable to defend themselves—forced to stand there while they were stripped of their valuables by these trigger-anxious killers!

A panic was inevitable, women screaming, fainting, being trampled underfoot; men desperately trying to help them. That would be the signal for the guns to go into action. The slaughter down there beneath the surface of the streets would be too awful to contemplate.

In some way that monstrous scheme must be spiked, crushed—but how? Single-handed, how could he possibly hope to cope with the hundreds, perhaps thousands, who were at that very moment gathered in all parts of the city, ready for the signal to loose on their victims?

The police were the only hope. In same way Wentworth must reach a telephone and get in touch with headquarters. Sanford Dane would *have* to heed and take action to thwart this shocking outrage. But how could he possibly get to a telephone—slip out of this guarded building?

The guard at the door... That would be easy, inspiration whispered quickly. The problem was to evade these others so as to be able to reach him. Half a dozen times Wentworth tried to edge his way out of the crowd, then had to turn back because watchful, suspicious eyes were upon him. Precious minutes slipped past. The time was getting shorter, shorter. At last he reached the corridor and hurried down its length—to face the mean, hostile eyes of the alert guard.

"Where in hell you think you're goin?" the gunman demanded threateningly.

"Going out for you," Wentworth said easily. "If I can find a phone, I'll get in touch with a party who will have the stuff for you—as soon as we finish with this job. Got to reach him now or he'll be gone—then I won't able to contact him till tomorrow."

The threat of being cut off from his drug supply for another day was too much for the guard. He stepped aside and Wentworth hurried past. The nearest telephone booth was two blocks away. Wentworth reached it in record time and put through a call to headquarters. The pompous, sonorous voice of Acting Commissioner Sanford Dane came over the wire.

"This is a warning, Dane," Wentworth said crisply. "Never mind who I am—just listen. At five o'clock the subways are going to be held up by an army of crooks. All three systems. Trains leaving all the main express stations will be stopped, robbed. Act quickly and you may prevent a panic that will cost thousands of lives."

"Who is this? Tell me who you are," Dane demanded. "I am not accustomed to listening to anonymous telephone calls—not even from you, Spider!" he finally snapped.

"For once in your life you are right, Dane," Wentworth admitted. "This is the Spider. I'm giving you a tip that may save your job. God help you if you're pig-headed enough to ignore it!"

"So you want me to send hundreds of my men down into the subways so that your killers can slaughter them?" Dane countered. "You want me to help you build up your Green Death reputation?"

Into Wentworth's mind flashed a reminder of the police who had *not* died when they raided Blinky McQuade. That gave him a hunch.

"That is exactly what I do not want you to do, Dane," he answered. "The men who normally would answer the riot calls are doomed if they respond today. Keep them away from the subways. Put in a call for the reserves from the Bronx and Brooklyn. Rush them to Manhattan as fast as you can, and let them handle the job. Meanwhile you can contact the transportation companies and have the motormen warned at all the stations."

"I don't know why I should trust you, Spider." Dane's voice sounded doubtful, half-convinced. "If I could be sure… If there is some way that you can prove what you say.…"

Wentworth hung up and hurriedly left the booth before his call could be traced. Sanford Dane was so pitifully obvious when he believed himself clever.…

Dane was a stubborn fool; no question about that. But would he be stupid enough to ignore such a warning? Wentworth did not know, and hated to gamble on the man's uncertain mental processes. There must be something else that he could do, someone else whom he could reach. The only one he could think of was Jim Mack. If Mack knew of this impending hold-up, he would act quickly.

On the way back to the factory Wentworth stopped in a tiny candy and stationery store, purchasing a sheet of writing paper and an envelope. He wrote a brief note, acquainting Mack with the situation, signed it 'Casimir Belotti' and addressed it to the detective at the Bowery lodging-house. The store proprietor had a son who jumped at the chance of earning five dollars for delivering it.

Now the problem was to get back into the factory. The time was almost expired; the gangsters must be about ready to start—and Wentworth could only hope that his absence had not been noticed. Quickly he retraced his steps and entered the side door.

"Okay, everything fixed," he grinned as he faced the guard. But something in those mean little rat eyes warned him of danger….

SUDDENLY THE gunman strode across the intervening space and grabbed Wentworth by his left hand, whipped it around so that the palm was up, stared down at it—then raised murder-glinting eyes to Wentworth's face.

"So, you dirty punk—you're a phony!" he snarled. "Deuce always calls me Dink—and you don't call me nothin'. I noticed that before. And Deuce Behrman has a scar inside his hand where a knife sliced him—"

His right hand was streaking for his gun, but his left still had hold of Wentworth's hand… and that was his undoing. Before he could release his grip, his fingers were imprisoned in a steely vise. His arm was twisted backward, over his shoulder—in a hold that sent agony stabbing through his left side. He whipped around with his automatic, and a warning yell burst from his lips… a yell that would bring the rest of the gang.

It was too late for Wentworth to flee; they would shoot him

down before he reached the corner. His only chance was to bluff it out... and the more sensational the bluff the better.

The gunman's yell stopped in mid-cry as Wentworth's gun barrel smashed down on his skull—hard-driving blows that splintered the bone. In a flash Wentworth wiped the blood from the barrel on the inside of the killer's coat and bent over the blood-drenched face to stamp his forehead with the Spider's crimson seal. Feet were pounding down the corridor now, men yelling excitedly. But Wentworth shouted a curse and triggered his gun. Flinging open the side door, he fired twice more as he ran and had reached the street end of the driveway before he turned back to face the pack that came boiling out after him.

"He got away!" he spat his disgust. "Had a car waiting for him out there at the curb. I put a couple bullets in it, but not enough to stop him—the dirty rat!"

Now Blackie Leahy came striding forward, gun in hand, the deep roach of his black hair squinted down so low that it almost reached the bridge of his nose.

"What are you doing out here, Behrman?" he demanded. "How come you got out here so much quicker than the others?"

"Because I was wise to that bird—and didn't have sense enough to clip him when I had the chance." Wentworth grimaced. "I saw him edging over toward the hallway and followed him out to Dink. Before I could reach them, he gave it to Dink. I almost got him when he stamped that thing on Dink's head, but he threw himself on the floor and went out the door like a damn crab."

Leahy's dark eyes narrowed. "What did this guy look like?" he asked curtly.

"Just an ordinary-looking guy—sorta dark, with a beak of a nose you couldn't miss," Wentworth described. "His clothes weren't any too hot; looked like he's slept in them."

But Leahy wasn't listening to him. He turned and faced the shifty-eyed gang in the alley. The name of the Spider and that crimson imprint on a dead man's face had had their effect. Some were muttering.

"Seems like we had the Spider here spying on us," Leahy confronted them. "So what? The hell with him! I don't want any of you guys getting cold feet on account of that. What can the Spider do to stop us? Nothing. We're going through with this whether the Spider knows about it or not. That's all. Get into your cars."

But Wentworth had a shrewd hunch that that was not all, so far as Blackie Leahy was concerned. Leahy didn't like the look of Dink's death, but there was nothing he could put his finger on to confirm his half-formed suspicions. He had to accept "Behrman's" story. Wentworth noticed him talking to Tony Rinaldi, a well known killer who was listed in the same crew as himself, and knew what that meant. He was to be "eliminated" at an opportune moment in the coming fracas....

THE CREW to which Wentworth was assigned was delegated to take care of the second downtown express that left the Brooklyn Bridge station after their arrival. At the station, Leahy eyed his wristwatch until five-twenty. Then he gave the word, and his thugs began filtering down onto the platforms, easing their way through the crowd.

Wentworth was one of the sack-men with the rear-of-the-train party. Instantly he noticed that instead of the regulation six men, seven gangsters formed his crew. Seven… temporarily. With difficulty they wedged their way through the close-packed car to the rear platform and had barely reached their places when the train began to move. Tensely the seven of them waited, the gunmen ready to unsheathe their weapons, the sack-men to open the heavy canvas bags they carried under their coats.

But two of those seven waited for something more than that—Wentworth and Tony Rinaldi. Wentworth kept a careful watch on his companion. He detected the tell-tale gleam of the born killer in the thug's eyes; caught his fleeting half-glance. The train slowed down, came to a stop.

"Now!" the crew leader said softly. His guns came out of their holsters and jammed into the backs of two citizens. "Get 'em up in the air!" his voice lashed out in the suddenly hushed car. "This is a stick-up! Don't try to pull anything, any of you, or—"

The rest of his threat was blotted out by a roar of shots—and the crowd's gasp as a body dropped to the platform. Tony Rinaldi had made a lightning-swift draw, but the bullet that had been meant for Wentworth merely smashed harmlessly into the roof of the car.

Wentworth still held the canvas bag in his hand. Now there was a bullet hole in the bottom—and another in the center of Rinaldi's forehead! Before the corpse hit the floor, Wentworth went into swift action.

It was too dangerous to attempt further gunplay in that humanity-packed car, but now his automatics had become clubs. Right and left they flailed out over the heads of the gunmen. Two went down—then another. The remaining two closed in on him, bore him to the floor—but one died there with a bullet in his brain. The other swung viciously at Wentworth's head as they got to their knees, struck him a glancing blow that hurled him back against the rear of the car.

Had the thug followed his advantage, Wentworth's fate would have been sealed. But all the gunman thought of was getting away. Like a pursued rabbit, he dived into the thick of the terrified passengers.

In the space of a few moments that crowded car had become a madhouse—a hive of screaming, struggling men and women. Frenziedly they tore at one another, trying to escape from that lethal struggle. Women shrieked and fainted; men cursed and fought. Dozens lost their footing and brought others to the floor on top of them; were trampled there before they could get back to their feet. Windows smashed. In the midst of the struggle somebody worked the mechanism that opened the side doors— to spill a score of screaming, floundering victims out onto the dark tracks and the deadly third rail.

Richard Wentworth's great heart was wrung with pity as he witnessed that panic-stricken riot; but there was nothing he could do to stem it. He could only hope to prevent its repetition in the nine or ten cars ahead.

LEAPING BACK over the prostrate bodies of the gunmen, he opened the rear door of the car, dropped out beside the track.

In the darkness he crouched in the deeper shadow of a pillar. There his expert fingers went to work with a speed they had never equalled—and in an incredibly short time his face was transformed. The black cape was over his shoulders, the floppy-brimmed hat fell low over his eyes.

Over the bed of the local track the Spider raced forward until he reached the first car of the express. There an uproar that rivaled the one at the rear raged a howling bedlam that completely drowned the noise of his footsteps. He ran to the motorman's window, hoisted himself up beside it. In his cubbyhole the motorman quailed, hands lifted in the air and a threatening gun muzzle no more than a foot from his stomach.

For an instant the Spider hesitated, loathe to take chances with an innocent man's life. But there was no alternative—nothing to do but work so fast that the gangster would not have time to pull the trigger. Full into the motorman's window he slapped his pistol muzzle—and fired through the tinkling glass as the weapon snapped to aim on the gunman's heart.

That shot added to the hysterical pandemonium in the car, but the motorman thought quickly. He whirled to meet the deliverer who had appeared as if by magic at his back, held out his hand and helped Wentworth through the window into the car.

The gunman, who had covered the motorman, had taken Blackie Leahy's instructions literally. The bullet-torn bodies of three men and a woman lay sprawled a few yards from him. Just out of reach of his clawed fingers were the guns that had dropped from his hands. Wentworth snatched them up and held them out to the motorman—a husky, gray-haired Irishman, who regarded him with popping eyes.

"You look like a fighter," Wentworth's voice was the discordant cackle of the Spider. "Are you game to follow me and take your train away from these murdering thieves?"

"I am—Spider!" the motorman gulped. "I always said you were better than all the cops in this city—now I know it. I'll follow you to hell!"

For an instant the Spider's hand rested on his shoulder in a clasp of commendation that John Terrence O'Mara was to remember and boast of for the rest of his life. Then they were off, the Spider in the lead, tunneling a way through the close-packed passengers who struggled back from their path as they approached.

"The Spider!" someone shouted. Suddenly the name became a glad cry of deliverance. It stilled the panic and helped men to get hold of themselves. "The Spider! That's the Spider with us!"

The roar of acclaim followed him into the second car; leaped ahead of him when he opened the closed door of the third. Here the looting thugs were at work. With snarls of rage, they whirled at the sudden interruption behind them. Then their guns froze in their hands, like props in the stiff fingers of wax-works dummies.

"Down! Down on the floor, you people!" the Spider croaked a warning.

Frantically the terror-maddened passengers fought to get out of the way of the barrage of bullets expected at any moment. Not until he was sure that they were safe did the Spider turn loose his guns. Now the crooks were in full flight. Desperately they triggered a scattered volley of shots at that dancing, weaving midnight apparition and the grim-faced, crouching motorman. But their main idea was to get as far as possible from the fearsome avenger who tracked them so implacably. They raced pell-mell for the doors at the end of the car, plunging through them, into the darkness between the tracks—just as the Spider's guns added two more to their toll.

Now the subway tunnels were echoing with the shriek of whistles calling vainly for aid. Wentworth realized that the other gunmen crews were meeting with more success than his own. Sanford Dane had not managed to warn the motormen or protect the trains, but perhaps his men were waiting at the stations. Perhaps the gangsters would find an unexpected reception committee on hand when they arrived with their loot.

The same idea must have been in Motorman O'Mara's mind.

"Is it all right if I get under way, sir?" he asked doubtfully, as he stared at the Spider's ugly visage and unmistakable costume.

"Perfectly," Wentworth nodded, "but first—"

He stepped into the motorman's cubbyhole and lithely vaulted out of the window, to drop safely into the darkness.

"God bless you, sir!" O'Mara called softly through the shattered window-pane as he grasped the controls and started the train on its interrupted trip to the Fulton Street station....

The moment Wentworth dropped to the subway floor he started to remove his makeup. Before he had trudged to the next station, the last vestige of the Spider was gone. Again it was in Deuce Behrman's garb, that Wentworth mingled with the passengers who swarmed to the Fulton Street station. By now the subway was jammed with stalled trains, ringing with hysterical screams and frantic calls for help. In single file the terrified passengers, who had deserted the cars, were making their way along the narrow walking space beside the track.

But when they climbed to the Fulton Street station platform the panic and confusion was as bad as it had been in the trains. Passengers from an earlier train which had been held up, had already reached the street level and spread the alarm. And the reserves from the nearest police station had answered in sudden and bewildering force.

On the platform of the station Wentworth saw them—on the stairway, upstairs on the street. They lay scattered in every direction, blue-coated men who were writhing in their death agonies while the ghastly hue of the Green Death spread over their stricken faces! Dozens of them! Wherever he looked, Wentworth saw the ravages of that terrible scourge. Bitterly he cursed Sanford Dane for not having kept those men away from the stations.

They had had no chance. Their deaths had been decreed even before they came leaping out of their squad cars....

Why was it, Wentworth wondered as he turned away from that scene of stark tragedy, that the police succumbed to the Green Death only under certain circumstances? Apparently the victims were doomed beforehand; before they even reached the scene of their death.

When the thieves clashed with the police on their own initiative, they ran into the same hard-fighting bluecoats that experience had taught them to expect. But when the Underworld hordes swarmed forth under the aegis of the Green Death, the police crumpled helplessly before them. There was something devilish about that. Wentworth grimly determined to discover the secret of this fiend's power over the forces of law and order— even though that meant bringing down the deadly blight upon himself!

CHAPTER 7
TERROR TRAIL

WENTWORTH REALIZED that it was useless to go back to the empty factory Blackie Leahy had used as a rendezvous. Undoubtedly the gangsters would have deserted it by now. If they did return to it, he would be powerless without the aid of the police. This aid he would never have now. For Sanford Dane had made the issue clear; he was warring on the Spider and blind to anything else. The Spider must carry on the battle against the Green Death, alone.

That meant that he must cover every angle himself, and one angle which demanded investigation was the peculiar one of Professor Stephen Thrall. Wentworth had given the Thrall situation deep thought and hit upon a way by which he might be able to contact the professor without arousing his suspicions. He went to a telephone booth and called Dr. Hugo Schoenheit.

"This is Richard Wentworth again, Doctor," he said when the physician's guttural voice answered, "calling about the little Hanley boy. How is he coming along?"

"Ach, I am glad you called me up, Mr. Wentworth," the old

German exclaimed, and Wentworth was quick to note the worry in his voice. "The last time you called, I told you the little boy was recovering slowly but was making a nice gain. That was what I thought then. But over-night his condition changed, and since then I have been able to do nothing with him. He has lost consciousness and lies in a coma. He is getting weaker, and I am afraid he will not live much longer.

"It is a strange case, Mr. Wentworth—very strange. He does not respond to any of my treatments. I have tried everything. If you think maybe you would like to place him under the care of some other doctor...."

"We'll talk about that, Doctor," Wentworth decided; "but not over the telephone. I shall be up to see you in a short while."

Bobby Hanley's illness would make even simpler the contact he contemplated, but Wentworth had no desire for that additional aid. He was filled with concern for the boy as he stopped at a secondhand store and bought a suit of clothing less flamboyant than Behrman's outfit. Again the make-up kit went into action. Now Wentworth had become an unimpressive, middle-aged man—a typical slightly grayed office worker who would attract a second glance from nobody.

Schoenheit, answered the bell, greeting him without a sign of recognition—until Wentworth spoke. Then the old physician quickly ushered his visitor inside and carefully locked the door after him.

"How is the boy now?" Wentworth asked.

"Not good—not good." Schoenheit shook his head puzzledly,

and then led the way to the bed where the little form lay stretched as immobile as a corpse.

As Wentworth looked down at the almost waxlike white features, he saw Ruth Hanley's anxious face in their stead; heard her voice pleading with him to see that the lad was cared for. And now it seemed that Bobby Hanley was about to follow his mother to the grave... For a moment Wentworth hesitated, debating whether he dare gamble with the child's life. But reason told him that what he planned was no gamble; Stephen Thrall was an expert brain specialist and surgeon.

"You know of Professor Stephen Thrall, Doctor?" He watched Schoenheit's face.

"*Ach*, but naturally," the German nodded. "Who does not? A great man who ruined a career that was of the most promising. He should be doing brilliant work now, but instead he is in prison."

"Not any longer, Doctor," Wentworth corrected. "He is free again; has a laboratory right here in the city. What would you think of him for this baby? Could we interest him in the case?"

Schoenheit demurred on ethical grounds, offered objections. Yet Wentworth saw that the idea appealed to him, that he only needed urging. Ten minutes later Schoenheit had contacted Professor Thrall by telephone and induced the scientist to receive them and examine the child.

MAIDA THRALL met them at the door of the old, somewhat shabby four-story brownstone building on East Twenty-seventh Street. Wentworth carried the boy inside to a laboratory where an examination table had been prepared. For a few minutes they waited, while the girl made small talk. With every probing glance at her pretty face, Wentworth became more certain of the suspicion that had assailed him the moment he beheld her.

This was the girl he had seen with the old man on Eighty-sixth Street—the night of the Yorkville massacre!

Now he was facing the man himself—the same high-boned, gaunt-cheeked, prominent-nosed face he had glimpsed in the sedan at Times Square when all of Broadway felt the scourge of the Green Death; the same aesthetic face, with its aureole of longish gray hair, that he had beheld in the midst of the Yorkville shambles!

Professor Thrall, who had claimed to be the Master of the Green Death, was the man of the strange Jekyll-Hyde face who had followed the carnage so promptly that first night when the Green Death had burst upon the startled metropolis!

Wentworth overcame his amazement and thrust aside the myriad questions that were clamoring to be answered. He watched the old man examine the stricken baby; saw the look of compassion dawn in the expressive face.

"You are quite right, Doctor Schoenheit," Thrall announced regretfully as he finished his diagnosis. "The child will not live more than perhaps forty-eight hours. The injury is internal; a brain lesion caused by the shock of the explosion."

"And there is nothing—nothing that you can do, Professor?" Schoenheit pressed.

For an instant the scientist hesitated, seemed to consider.

"There is only one chance of saving his life," he said then; "and that is by an extremely precarious operation—which I no longer have the right to perform. You forget that my license has been revoked. Unfortunately I know of nobody else who is qualified to undertake it."

"But what is a matter of a license when a life is at stake, Professor?" Wentworth protested quickly. "Surely you will not let this baby die when it lies within your power to save his life? We are entirely willing to accept complete responsibility—"

"If the operation should not be successful the responsibility will be entirely mine," Schoenheit interposed. "Nobody will ever know that you were in any way connected with the case."

But Stephen Thrall was wavering—and at last yielded.

"There must be one more who will know of this," he stipulated. "Doctor Spalding, who is helping me in some experiments. He will assist me with the ether. He is here in the building now. Call him, Maida."

Fifteen minutes later all was in readiness. In their white surgeon's gowns, faces half-hidden by gauze masks, Thrall and Howard Spalding stood beside the white table on which lay little Bobby Hanley. Schoenheit, also white-uniformed, stood by as an observer; Wentworth and Maida Thrall watched from the background.

With trephine and keen-bladed lancet, Stephen Thrall went to work, and before their eyes performed a masterpiece of surgery. Totally absorbed in his work, he seemed to forget that anyone else was present—appeared to retreat within himself and hold communion with his troubled spirit.

"Fools—fools!" he muttered softly. "Poor, benighted fools! It isn't enough that they took away six years of my life—still they must persecute me! I am no longer fit to practice. I can no longer operate—can no longer perform operations that nobody else can handle. That is their perverted idea of justice! Rob suffering humanity in order to punish a man who did no wrong—that is their hypocritical justice!"

His low-spoken words were clear and penetrating in the utter stillness of that operation room. Wentworth could not ignore them; could not help but see the agony of fear that welled up into Maida Thrall's eyes as she darted anxious glances at him.

"Don't worry, I understand," he whispered reassuringly. "I am the one you wanted to see—Richard Wentworth."

Her eyes widened at the mention of his name. The anxiety fled from her face, gave way to a look of satisfaction, almost of elation. Even before the operation was entirely completed she left the room, to return to the doorway a few minutes later and silently beckon him to follow. In the now lighted reception-room at the front of the building she sat down and faced him anxiously.

"I am so glad you came!" she blurted impulsively. "So glad that you could see him as he is tonight. There is nothing the matter with his mind; you saw that. His hand is skillful as ever. But he cannot seem to forget. He broods over what he has been through—even when he is concentrating most rigidly on his work. Doctor Spalding spends as much time as he can with him now. Between us we watch him so that—so that there will be no repetition of his visit to Mr. Kirkpatrick.

"That is one of the strangest things about him, Mr. Wentworth—he seems to have forgotten that visit entirely. He never has mentioned it; and several times when I tried to hint at it, tried to refer to it guardedly, he did not seem to have the least idea of what I meant. It is almost as if he has become two people—one of whom does not know what the other is doing. At times he terrifies me."

Once she was launched upon the subject of her father she became so voluble that Wentworth could not halt her. Even after the operation was finished and Dr. Schoenheit was waiting, ready to leave, she tried to detain him with a few whispered last-minute details. Yet she actually had little to add to the information she had given Nita. Wentworth did not doubt her sincerity and her anxiety, but there was nothing to be gained by listening to a mere recital of her fears.

THE HANLEY boy, it had been arranged, was to remain there under Thrall's care for several days. At last Wentworth managed to terminate the conversation. He started for the door—but the moment he and Schoenheit stepped out onto the high, second-floor stoop he felt that something was wrong. Twenty-seventh Street, almost empty of cars and pedestrians at that time of night, seemed normally deserted… yet he sensed the stare of spying eyes, felt the scrutiny of hidden ambushers waiting for him to walk into some trap.

And then he knew where they were!

The darkness on both sides of the high stoop sheltered crouching men pressed tightly against the walls of the buildings. Some barely perceptible movement in those deep shadows had registered on his subconscious mind and warned him. Now he saw that one of the lurking men was not entirely out of the patch of illumination from a nearby arc-light. Part of its beam revealed a tell-tale strip of blue cloth.

The police!

Schoenheit was saying something about the Hanley boy's condition, and Wentworth mumbled an indistinct answer— but his muscles were tensed, his skin fairly crawling. He started down the steps, expecting to feel the shock of a bullet in his back. Now he noticed a taxicab, a luxurious Packard, coming toward the building. The driver had seen them and was cruising in the hope of obtaining a fare.

Wentworth signaled. The driver was already swerving in toward the curb. He reached out to open the door, but still those ambushed policemen had made no move. Schoenheit was in front, just about to step through the doorway—when suddenly Wentworth jerked him aside so forcefully that he lost his balance, fell to the sidewalk.

In that instant the quiet street suddenly roared with life. Guns blazed redly from the darkness on both sides of the Thrall house, and policemen came charging out onto the sidewalk. Wentworth had hurled himself through the cab doorway, the moment Schoenheit was out of the way. Inside, he clutched automatics in both hands. A fraction of a second before the trap was sprung, he had spotted it; had glimpsed the hardly distinguishable form of a man crouched low on the seat against the cab's near side. Before that fellow had a chance to move Wentworth was upon him, jabbing both gun muzzles hard into the belly of—Jim Mack!

Jim Mack! How under heaven did he come to be there? Even in that moment of stunning surprise Wentworth made no slip.

"Out!" he ordered. One hand pressed down on the handle of the farther door, pushed it open. Jim Mack pitched head over heels out into the street!

Bullets were raining against the cab now, shattering the windows and pocking the metal body. Before the driver could desert his wheel, Wentworth pressed his guns against the fellow's neck.

"Drive!" Wentworth snapped.

"All right, mister!" the cabbie babbled. He got the machine under way just as Wentworth whipped a gun out of the side window and knocked a policeman off the running-board. "I didn't have nothin' to do with this, mister! I couldn't help myself! They come up and told me I had to do it!"

"Uptown—over to the West Side," Wentworth said. "Step on it."

The cabbie went to work, frantically. He turned, stepped his blocks, doubled back then darted ahead at break-neck speed. Wentworth was not thinking about any immediate destination. His thoughts were back at the Thrall house, reconstructing everything that had happened there—trying to account for that deadly trap which he had so narrowly escaped.

How had Jim Mack happened to be there with the police? Either he had managed to trail Wentworth somehow, or he had been summoned by someone in the Thrall building. But by whom? The only two persons there who knew Wentworth's identity were Schoenheit and Maida Thrall. Schoenheit was above suspicion. But the girl had been out of his sight for a few minutes after he divulged his identity... Long enough for her to have put through a call to the police.

Was that why she had detained him so persistently with her recital? Or could the informant have been Thrall or Howard Spalding? Could either of them have discovered his identity? Or had one of them eavesdropped on his conversation with Maida Thrall, and then called the police?

Hopelessly Wentworth gave up trying to answer those questions. The cab was running uptown along Eighth Avenue when he ordered the driver to turn into a side street and paid him off. Quickly Wentworth lost himself among the avenue crowd and then leisurely walked in the direction of Broadway. It was eleven-fifteen, and the rendezvous for which he was headed was not until twelve o'clock.

That rendezvous was designated by one of those cryptically worded personal column notices which had appeared in the morning newspapers. "Gideon Dubois" had ordered that the Green Death's percentage of the day's loot must be delivered before midnight at an address on West Forty-ninth Street which Wentworth had located between Sixth and Seventh Avenues. IT WAS eleven-thirty when he passed the designated building and saw that the ground floor was occupied by a small stationery-and-office equipment store. It was dark but Wentworth's keen eyes quickly spotted a mail-slit in the door and a large-sized box behind it. Farther up the block he crossed the street, to retrace his steps on the other side and slip into a hallway opposite the rendezvous. Now he could see that the rest of the building was also in darkness. It was a narrow, four-story structure which seemed occupied by tenants of no particular significance… until he spied the gold-lettered name of "Franklin Penney, Attorney at Law" on the three windows of the third floor.

Franklin Penney, the criminal lawyer… It was he who had been the prosecuting attorney in the Stephen Thrall case. That might be nothing but the merest coincidence, but now Wentworth was dismissing no possible tie-ups with Thrall, no possible leads to the Green Death….

He was still recalling what he knew about Franklin Penney, and debating where the glib "mouthpiece" might fit into the baffling criminal puzzle—when he saw a man approach the door of the dark stationery store and shove something through the mail chute. Within the next fifteen minutes, six more men had stopped to drop envelopes or small packages through the slit.

By ten minutes to twelve the last of the "depositors" seemed to have arrived. A lull followed, and Wentworth counted the minutes until midnight. At five after twelve another man arrived and stepped into the dark doorway, fitted a key to the lock and went inside.

Wentworth tensed. Now he saw that he had not been the only watcher whose eyes were glued on that dark storefront.

From the building next to the one in which he stood, another man stepped—a man whom he recognized as Franklin Penney! The attorney started across the street. As if his appearance was the signal that brought them forth, four other, gangster-type individuals came out of the side entrance of the building that housed the stationery store. They started for the dark store door-way. For a moment they crowded around the lock. Then they, too, went inside—and Wentworth caught the gleam of pistols in their hands.

For some reason Franklin Penney hesitated and remained just outside the doorway—which was all that saved his life.

Suddenly the nocturnal quiet was shattered by a thunderous explosion. The interior of the store was lit by a blinding flash. Then the show windows belched out into the street—and Franklin Penney was brushed off his feet and tumbled into the gutter.

Debris was still tumbling to the floor in clouds of dust, when a single man came out of that wrecked shop. It was the lone arrival who had been the first to enter it. Without so much as a glance at Penney, who was dazedly getting to his feet, the fellow turned on his heel and started walking toward Sixth Avenue. The night depository was finished doing business, and the collector was on his way back to headquarters—with Richard Wentworth close behind.

The collector carried his satchel to the corner, stepped into a cab. Fortunately another was right behind it. Wentworth slipped inside and ordered the driver to follow the first car. Crouched close to the window, he saw that the trail was leading back to the east side of the city. He stared in amazement when the lead cab turned left on East Twenty-eighth Street and stopped at an office building that must have been directly in back of the Thrall residence on Twenty-seventh!

The collector paid off his driver, turned into the dimly night-lighted entrance of the building without a glance in either direction. A queer individual who moved with the precision of a robot. He had passed the elevator shaft and was heading for the stairway beyond, when Wentworth cat footed up to him—and leaped upon his back.

For a moment the collector attempted to struggle. But Wentworth's fist flashed out and connected with the point of his jaw in an uppercut that lifted him off his feet—then dropped him, senseless, to the floor.

Again, in that brief struggle, Wentworth had had the peculiar feeling that he was battling not with a human being but with an automaton, an uncomprehending dummy. The man seemed to have no sense of what he was doing; no emotion whatever was reflected in his peculiarly blank face and dull, lackluster eyes....

Swiftly Wentworth glanced around the empty hallway. The elevators were not running, and there seemed to be no night watchman or guard to look after the door. The building was utterly quiet and seemed to be empty. But he must be certain. The stairway toward which the collector had been headed led both upstairs and also down into the basement. Wentworth decided upon the upper floor. Swinging the inert body over his shoulder and grabbing up the heavy, loot-filled satchel, he trudged his way up.

The hallway there was completely dark. Dropping the unconscious man to the floor, he quickly stripped off the fellow's suit and necktie and donned them in place of his own. Next he removed the collector's shirt and tore it into strips with which he bound his captive's ankles and wrists and tightly secured the handkerchief gag between his slack jaws.

That dull, blank-looking countenance was simple to counterfeit. Wentworth played his flashlight over the commonplace, undistinguished features then went to work with his makeup kit. In a few minutes he was certain that he looked sufficiently like a show-window clothes' dummy to impersonate the fellow anywhere.

The next question was—where had the collector been going with his loot? Wentworth picked up the heavy satchel and started down the stairs to investigate the lower floor more thoroughly. He was halfway down when his hand froze on the banister. The door downstairs had opened, and another arrival was crossing the lower corridor!

Just in time he drew back noiselessly into the darkness and watched. The new satchel-toting collector passed the elevators and came on toward the stairs. Again Wentworth stared almost unbelievingly, while an eerie chill played up and down his spine. For a moment Wentworth had the queer feeling that he was looking at the man he had knocked out and left tied up on the floor above!

The same blank-looking face, same suit and hat, same tie… They must be twins; must be deliberately supplementing their similarity with identical clothing….

The collector turned into the darkness beyond the elevator shaft, walked to the steps that led down to the cellar. Wentworth waited until he was halfway down the flight, then softly cat footed his way to the main floor and back to the cellar stairs.

His unsuspecting guide led him into a large basement that was piled high with discarded machinery—and suddenly seemed to vanish among the grotesque heaps. But when Wentworth followed, he discovered a narrow canyon that wound its way through the rusty assemblage and brought him to a well hidden door in the stone wall.

Beyond that door was a long, dimly lighted tunnel that seemed to stretch onward endlessly into the earth. Wentworth plodded along through it in the same mechanical fashion as the man who was just disappearing at its farther end... until suddenly he turned a sharp corner and stepped out into another basement where more than a dozen of those amazing blank-faced duplicates were assembled!

Like inanimate dummies they sat hunched on benches that were grouped around a huge, flat-topped desk now piled with the loot satchels. At a desk sat Professor Stephen Thrall, totaling the proceeds of the day's outrages! More than a dozen men stared at Stephen Thrall with lack-luster faces in which only the eyes were expressive—burning eyes that were filled with a mingling of bitter hate and feverish hope!

CHAPTER 8
THE BLANK-FACED MEN

QUIET LITTLE Livingstonville, in the northern foot-hills of the Catskill Mountains, was a charming village. John Bouck did not question that—but it offered absolutely no opportunity for a young man who wanted to make money.

Money had not mattered so much to him until he met Julie Metcalf and realized that she was the only girl in the world for him. Then it became a matter of supreme importance—the only thing that stood between him and his wedding day.

That was why John Bouck came to New York.

"I'll find a job down there and save up enough to get us started off right. Then I'll come up here and take you back with me," he promised Julie the morning he kissed her good-bye and took the bus to the city.

But before he had been in New York a fortnight he realized that his ambitious program might have to be considerably delayed....

He had had fifty dollars when he arrived in the city, but that had dwindled with remarkable rapidity. Before it was entirely gone he gave up his inexpensive furnished room and moved into a miserable hole-in-the-wall place on the lower East Side that called itself a hotel. It was there that he finally took the drink that was his undoing.

Bouck had been badly discouraged that night. When the manager, coming to his room for the weekly rent, suggested that a drink might cheer him up, he gladly accepted a generous helping from the proffered bottle.

The whiskey warmed him pleasantly as it went down... but the trouble was that the warmth did not stop there. It increased steadily, until his stomach felt like a roaring furnace and his whole body seemed to be on fire. Perspiration was pouring off him as he dropped to the floor and rolled in agony. Somehow he managed to get his door open and called for help; begged the gaping roomers to get him a doctor or send for an ambulance to take him to a hospital.

The manager himself attended to that. But instead of waiting for an ambulance, he took Bouck in a private car—took him to a private hospital where he was placed in the alcoholic ward. Yet no matter what the doctors did for him there, the frightful burning grew steadily worse until he knew that he was raving like a madman....

Perhaps he was mad—he didn't know. That terrible searing agony was enough to drive anyone out of his head. He was not surprised when he hazily heard a doctor declare that he was insane and would have to be removed to a sanitarium.

Insane? No, suddenly he knew that he *wasn't* insane; he was only half-mad with pain. He tried to explain that, but nobody paid any attention. Vaguely he realized that something queer was happening to him. These white-uniformed men were taking advantage of his helplessness in some way that he did not comprehend. But he was too ill to do anything about it. He heard the doctor say something about "commitment papers" as he took out his fountain-pen and prepared to sign an official-looking document.

John Bouck knew what commitment papers meant. Once they were signed, he might spend the rest of his life in an insane asylum. The knowledge stabbed through his pain-induced indifference and gave him the strength to fight desperately. But the white-uniformed men put a quick stop to that. They overwhelmed him and held him flat while he was strapped up tightly in a strait-jacket....

After that they shot something into him with a hypodermic syringe; and he knew nothing more until he woke and found himself lying on an operating table. He was strapped down helplessly, held in place so rigidly that he could not even move his head. A gray-haired old man with a large, sharp nose and wicked-looking eyes was bending over him, grinning down at him with an expression on his face that chilled Bouck from head to foot. The old man wore a surgeon's white uniform. Beside him was a porcelain tray on which was stretched a terrifying array of brightly polished surgical knives....

"Ah, so you are awake," the surgeon nodded approvingly. "That is better. I can work much more satisfactorily when I can note the reactions."

He reached for one of the knives... and what went on after that became a ghastly nightmare of horror and pain for John Bouck; a hellish ordeal that finally ended when merciful blackness engulfed him....

BOUCK WAS never the same after that. When he recovered consciousness his face was swathed in bandages and it was agony to move a muscle. Days later they took off the last of the bandages. When he looked into a mirror, he no longer recognized himself—could hardly distinguish himself from the weird fraternity of *blank-faced* men into which he had been inducted.

Dazed with the horror of what had happened to him, it was some time before thought of resistance or escape occurred. But very soon he learned that he had no more will-power of his own; learned that he could do only what he was told. He was a prisoner, a captive without visible chains, held at the mercy of that malignant-eyed old man whom he heard the others call "Professor."

Daily the Professor examined him and shot a hypodermic injection into his arm. What that injection was, Bouck had no idea. Yet, the first time he attempted to disobey he learned its effect. That day he was locked up in a tiny cell of a room, and the Professor did not come near him. Tender thoughts of Julie Metcalf coursed through his mind during the hours while he sat and waited to see what would happen; thoughts which stiffened his determination to resist, no matter what they might do to him.

That was before the burning started again. The first hot wave that crept through him brought out a cold perspiration. Then the fire at the pit of his stomach kindled, flared higher, until the flames of hell were raging within him. Bouck screamed and yelled; he pounded on his door and frantically begged for relief… but the Professor did not come. Naked, he rolled and squirmed on the floor, frenziedly seeking relief. But there was no relief from that excruciating torture. The flames grew hotter, until it seemed that his whole body must be consumed by the inner conflagration.

Hours and hours of that frightful torture, he endured. When the Professor finally came with his hypodermic, Bouck hardly had the strength to crawl to the old man's feet and inarticulately beg for relief.

After that John Bouck knew that the Professor was his master. If anything happened to the old man, he was doomed to a living death—the tortures of hell on earth. Any disobedience would deprive him of the periodic injections which were the only means of averting the frightful spasms now his lot at regular intervals.

John Bouck did not forget Julie Metcalf; she was in his thoughts continually. But now it was as if she were dead, as if he had laid her in her grave and had turned away to face life alone. Now he knew that their dreams were ended because he never could return to her. In place of their ambitious plans, he had only a bitter, all-consuming hatred—a festering hatred about which he could do nothing.

That was John Bouck's life until one night when something leaped upon him and almost strangled him... until something exploded inside his head and he knew no more....

RICHARD WENTWORTH stared in astonishment at that basement congregation of blank-faced men and their demoniacal-looking master. Now he saw that they were not twins, were not as identical as he had first supposed. They were all dressed alike; they all shared that dull, lackluster expression—and something more. Yes, some sort of unholy operation must have been performed on them to reduce their features to a nearly common denominator of vacuity; an operation that had deprived them of their personalities and turned them into blank-faced zombies....

He caught himself up quickly when he saw that Thrall's piercing gaze was directed toward him. That momentary halt at the basement doorway had almost been his undoing, but Wentworth retrieved himself swiftly. Stepping forward mechanically, he placed his satchel on the desk. The suspicious glower in the old man's eyes gave way to an avaricious gleam. Eagerly he unlocked the receptacle and poured out on the desk twenty-five or thirty heavy, money-bulging envelopes and packages.

Accepted as one of the collectors, Wentworth now stepped back and took a seat on one of the benches with his blank-faced companions. They paid no attention to him nor to one another. Their whole world seemed to center in the old man who hunched over his desk, sorting out bundles of currency and bags of coins—totaling the results in a ledger spread beneath the desk light.

So Stephen Thrall had not been boasting idly when he claimed to be the Master of the Green Death… Mad he might very well be, but there was no doubt of the man's bloody-handed guilt. That money he was counting so eagerly had been garnered for him at the cost of hundreds of lives, of untold grief and misery….

Unobtrusively Wentworth started to edge his way along the bench, nearer and nearer to Thrall. If he could get close enough to the desk he might take advantage of the other's greedy preoccupation and spring upon him. Closer he edged—until suddenly he realized that such an attempt would be hopeless.

Not until then had he noticed the narrow slits which pierced the shadowy walls at intervals. Through those slits the muzzles of weapons projected—tommy-guns and repeating-rifles that were trained on him and would cut him down before he could hope to reach the desk. The Professor evidently was taking no chances even here in his underground stronghold.

Before Wentworth had an opportunity to evolve other strategy, there came an interruption that aroused even his lacka-daisical companions. Suddenly the tunnel through which he had recently passed, reverberated with a terrific howling—the agonized screaming of a soul in torment! Mutely the blank-faced men turned their gaze toward the doorway. Behind his desk, the gray-haired oldster half rose, an automatic clutched in his right hand. His face twisted into a mask of bleak rage as he hovered there like a demon in his own private hell.

Wentworth tensed—and in another moment what he feared, had happened. Through the doorway came another of the blank-faced men, dragging the bound, writhing figure of the man he had knocked out and left in the second-floor hallway! Now the exposure of his masquerade would be only a matter of minutes....

Even in that moment of his own peril, Wentworth stared pityingly at the awful agony that was revealed in the man's distorted face and twitching, convulsed body. He was enduring the tortures of the damned....

"So we have an impostor among us," Thrall backed away, covering them all with his automatic. "That is very unfortu-nate—for the foolish one who had no better sense than to intrude here. Bring him to me." He nodded to the screaming man on the floor; and two of the blank-faced men lifted their stricken companion and carried him forward.

From a drawer of the desk Thrall took a hypodermic syringe and a bottle that was nearly filled with a venomous-looking greenish liquid. The needle stabbed into the writhing man's arm, the barrel emptied into his veins. In a few moments his frantic struggles ceased and he began to subside, weak and perspiration-soaked from his ordeal.

"Now I shall attend to the rest of you." Thrall grimaced at the others. "Perhaps, before I am finished, we shall know which of you has no business here among us."

One by one they stepped forward and raised their sleeves for the injection. One by one… and with each Wentworth knew that his own time was growing shorter. He held back as long as he could. At last there was no alternative; he was the only one who had not been treated, and Thrall's eyes turned on him wolfishly.

To refuse to submit would be to confess his bogus identity. But to walk up there and bare his arm would mean to receive an injection of—what? The poison that had turned these men into mere automatons? Perhaps the very essence of the Green Death, to which these underlings had been immunized!

Now he could hold back no longer. Thrall had rapped out an order to bring him forward, and the others were closing in on him. Wentworth tensed, waited until they were almost upon him. Then he hurled himself forward in a desperate attempt to reach the old man.

But they were too many for him. They overwhelmed him, pinioned his arms before he could draw a gun, dragged him down and almost smothered him as they piled on top.

WENTWORTH STRUGGLED furiously, but their dazed condition seemed to have no impairing effect upon their strength. They held onto him firmly, lifted him and started forward to where Thrall waited with the loaded syringe. Wentworth could do no more. In another moment he would feel the sting of the needle, the surge of the green concoction as it spurted into his veins… Then, just as he was about to give up all hope, an amazing interruption occurred.

Wild-eyed and with fists flailing, the underwear-clad man he had knocked out came charging to his rescue! Desperately the fellow hurled himself upon his blank-faced mates and drove them back by the berserk fury of his unexpected charge….

When Wentworth's fist had connected with the point of John Bouck's jaw in the office building hallway, he had done more than knock the collector out. That jarring blow had done something to Bouck's dazed brain; had let in a bit of light through the drug fumes which veiled and clouded it. Now, as the burning agony subsided after the injection Thrall gave him, the effects of that blow were still with him.

For the first time in weeks Bouck was able to think clearly—to understand what had happened to him and what lay ahead. This man who was struggling there on the floor, he realized suddenly, was his only hope of escape, his only chance for life. The fearful burning spells to which he was subject had been unendurable. But if he could reach a doctor, he might be able to secure injections similar to those the Professor gave him… He could never hope to do that by himself, but with this man to aid him….

John Bouck was fighting not for Wentworth but for himself, for himself and for Julie Metcalf, when he charged into the blank-faced men and swept them aside. That accounted for the desperate savagery of his onslaught—for the way he drove them back and cleared a path.

Twice Thrall fired into the struggling pack. But his bullets only brought down his own men and the guns in the walls remained strangely silent. Dummies probably, Wentworth concluded as he broke loose from the clawing hands of the blank-faced men and dived into the tunnel doorway with his amazing rescuer. Back through the long passageway they raced. There seemed to be no pursuit, Wentworth noticed, when he flung a glance back over his shoulder. But just as they reached the dark basement of the Twenty-eighth Street office building, the tunnel echoed with a woman's shrill scream of terror.

That scream was Nita's! Wentworth recognized it instantly— and instinctively he stopped his flight. Nita was back there in the hands of that mad, murderous fiend! Nita—a helpless victim under that devilish hypodermic needle!

The inhuman devil was using her as bait for a trap. Wentworth's fists clenched and his lips compressed into a hard, tight line. He whirled, started back... But before he had gone more than three steps, the whole earth seemed to explode! A terrific detonation boomed through the tunnel. Wentworth was knocked off his feet by the concussion—and then the tunnel came tumbling in behind him!

Just in time he scrambled to his feet and got away from beneath the falling roof. A moment later the passageway was effectively sealed by tons of debris... and Nita was there at the other end of it!

THE WAY back through the tunnel was blocked, but there

131

was still the Thrall house on Twenty-seventh Street. Wentworth ran upstairs and out into the street, started for the Thrall
place… then remembered the blank-faced man who had helped
him to escape. What had happened to him? He had been in the
lead when Nita screamed; had been well clear when the explosion destroyed the tunnel. Wentworth looked up and down the
street—then saw him running toward the corner.

John Bouck's flash of normalcy had passed. On its heels came
a rush of terrible fear. He had to flee; had to escape from this
man who would take him away from the Professor and subject
him to endless hours of that excruciating torture! Wildly he
raced through the dark street, frantically casting about for a
place to hide.

Suddenly he seemed to disappear into nowhere. But as Wentworth rounded the corner and headed for Twenty-seventh
Street, he realized that his astonishing rescuer must have dived
down a manhole into a sewer!

The Thrall house was dark and peaceful looking when Wentworth came running up to it. The placid exterior did not deceive
him; not after what he had witnessed in his basement. A ready
gun was clutched in the left pocket of his coat when he rang the
bell. His right hand was ready for an instantaneous draw the
moment the door opened.

Maida Thrall answered the bell. She gazed at him with no
sign of recognition and admitted him doubtfully when he asked
to see her father on a matter of great urgency.

"It's rather late," she demurred, "but it happens that he is still awake. I don't know whether he can see you. He is with a patient now—a little boy who is very ill—"

"Never mind that," Wentworth clipped, and his gun covered the girl the moment they were inside. "I want to see him—now. And you are taking me to him—not bringing him here."

She gasped as the gun pressed close against her. Then her lips closed firmly, her eyes mirrored her contempt. Without a word she turned and led the way toward the rear of the building. Close on her heels, Wentworth followed her into the little bedroom just off the laboratory at the back of the second floor. There he found Stephen Thrall sitting beside the little bed in which Bobby Hanley lay sleeping.

The old man held up his hand for silence as they approached, then got up and came out into the laboratory with them.

"I think he will be all right now," he said softly. "It has been touch and go for the past three hours, but now he has passed the crisis—"

Only then did he seem to see the stranger whom his daughter had brought in. He looked at Wentworth inquiringly.

"This is a gentleman who called to see you—with a gun," Maida Thrall explained icily.

But Wentworth made no apologies. "You mean to say you have been here with that youngster for the past three hours?" he demanded. "Just here on this floor and not—let us say, in the cellar?" He was narrow-eyed.

Stephen Thrall looked utterly bewildered; glanced from Wentworth to his daughter, as if to find an explanation of the riddle in her eyes. "Certainly, I was here. But I do not see why

I should be expected to account for my movements to you. Who—"

"That will do," Wentworth cut him short, and now both guns were uncovered in his hands. "I want to have a look at this place—from top to bottom. You will come with me," he ordered.

Meekly they obeyed. Door after door Maida Thrall opened for him, while her father, hovering at her side, mumbled about police persecution.

From roof to cellar Wentworth searched that building. Nowhere could he find anything that resembled the basement room; any evidence of the tunnel doorway; nor so much as a trace of the blank-faced men... and nowhere could he find Nita. All that had disappeared as if it had been a dream.

Twice he went over every foot of the basement floor, testing it for a trapdoor that might lead to a sub-cellar. But there was nothing. Then the whistle of fire engines and the wail of police sirens told him that he had better leave, before another trap was baited outside. The Thrall house, he admitted, was a ghastly puzzle that had him stumped....

When he reached the corner he saw that people were running toward Twenty-eighth Street. Additional fire apparatus was converging on the street. By the time he joined the throng held back by the police, the entire lower floor of the office building was a roaring inferno that wiped out all hope of investigating its secrets.

Baffled, Wentworth turned away. On Twenty-third Street he located a telephone booth and tried what he knew was a forlorn hope. He called Nita's apartment. But the voice of old Jenkyns, his butler, came over the wire with the message he had feared. Nita was not there… had not been in all evening.

Her scream, at least, had been no part of a dream. Nita was in the hands of the Master of the Green Death….

CHAPTER 9
CITY OF NO LAW

NEW YORK CITY shuddered with horror the next morning when the full story of the subway hold-ups became known. That unpunished outrage was followed in the next few days by dozens of brazen criminal forays. Hourly, conditions in the metropolis grew worse. The Underworld, now completely freed from fear of police interference, ran absolutely wild; and the terrified citizenry called in vain for protection.

There was no safety in the five boroughs. Banks were looted, stores raided, theaters held up. Hotels, business offices, apartment houses, churches—all were invaded and looted at the point of pistols and tommy-guns. No man's property was secure from the gangs of hoodlums that roamed the streets. At home, one's valuables were a prey to burglars; on one's person there was the constant danger of losing them to hold-up men, who plied their trade with impunity.

Vainly the taxpayers appealed to Sanford Dane for relief. Vainly the business men protested against the staggering amount of extortion they were forced to pay in order to keep their doors open. The acting police commissioner issued bombastic statements which were supposed to be reassuring. But his men were powerless to protect anyone from the threat of the green crepe that had now become a symbol of certain death when the demands of the extortioners were not promptly met.

Looted of millions of dollars daily, New York was on the brink of chaos. There seemed no hope of relief....

At the end of a futile week, the Spider was almost ready to admit that he was beaten. Frantic with concern for Nita, he had hunted everywhere. She had disappeared—and leaving only that terrified scream ringing in his ears....

Equally thoroughly he had sought a lead to the Master of the Green Death—with as little success. Even the newspaper method of communicating with his gangster minions had been changed. Now Wentworth had nothing whatever to follow—nothing but Stephen Thrall, who seemed such an exemplary being.

Nightly Wentworth tucked his violin under his arm as Casimir Belotti, and made his round of the East Side bars and restaurants. He strained his ears for every scrap of conversation while his bow brought forth soft, haunting melodies. Finally his vigilance was rewarded....

He was playing in the back room of a bar, and had just passed a table where a man and a flashy-looking young woman were sitting and drinking, when their conversation caught at his attention. He cast a glance over his shoulder and quickly recognized the dark-eyed, swarthy-skinned, flat-featured man—Monte Pelano, a notorious killer whom Franklin Penney had "sprung" in a sensational trial less than a month ago.

"That fiddler reminds me," Pelano said softly, as he leaned

over the table closer to his companion. "That brother of yours is playing in one of the uptown hotspots, ain't he?"

"Chico? Sure," the girl nodded her yellow head. "He's with Bill Bode's band in the Shingle. Only he's no fiddler; he's a sax."

"Lot o' good that'll do him," Pelano shrugged. "Take a tip and tell him to stay away from there tomorrow night—check in sick or get plastered or somethin'. The night spots ain't going to be so healthy."

"What is it, Monte?" the girl pressed eagerly. "A stick-up? A scrap? What's coming off up there? Is the Green Death—"

But Pelano drew back to his own side of the booth table and froze up, his face an inscrutable mask.

"I ain't saying nothin'," he clipped. "I shouldn't have opened my yap. Thought you had enough sense to take a tip without having to have a diagram. Forget about it—see?"

He glanced around him uneasily. But Wentworth was now two booths away, beginning a request rendition of *My Wild Irish Rose*. His thoughts were busy with what he had just overheard. The night clubs would not be healthy tomorrow night… Saturday night, the biggest of the week… Probably a concerted raid on most of the largest places just as the theaters had been held up, simultaneously.

The night clubs… They were dangerous places for him because the police were keeping a sharp lookout there, confident that Richard Wentworth would eventually drop into one. But there was a way in which he could avoid their surveillance.

Tex Baker, orchestra leader at the Metropolitan Casino, the largest and most luxurious of the after-dinner establishments, was a friend who could be counted upon to do anything for Nita. If the night clubs were to be raided, the swanky Metropolitan Casino was certain to be visited by the hold-up men.

Promptly at closing hour Wentworth called the Casino and got Tex Baker on the telephone.

"This is Richard Wentworth, Tex," he introduced. "I—"

"You, Dick! Where are you?" Baker's surprised response came quickly in a low, guarded voice. "You need help…?"

"Not for myself, Tex—for Nita," Wentworth explained. "She has been missing for nearly a week. Here's what I'd like you to do. I will send you a man—Casimir Belotti—who is an expert violinist. He's good enough to be a concert player. I want him to be in the Metropolitan tomorrow night—in a position where he can watch the place without being conspicuous. Your orchestra platform is the best place for that. Let him sit in and play with you tomorrow night."

"Right," Baker agreed readily. "He doesn't even have to play if he doesn't want to; he can just dummy-saw. I'll be expecting him."

CASIMIR BELOTTI was on hand at the Metropolitan Casino early the next night, and Tex Baker breathed more easily when he saw him. He had feared that the man might turn out to be a burly, beef-necked detective who would look entirely out of place among the musicians. But Belotti was the sort of man who belonged in evening attire. His shadowy eyes, longish cheeks and indefinably foreign appearance added to his appeal and made him a distinct addition to the ensemble.

That was before Baker had heard him play. After that, the

leader gave up all idea of having his "guest artist" dummy-saw. Casimir Belotti was a natural musician, and Baker wondered why the man wasted his life working as a detective....

Wentworth watched the audience carefully. Between each number his practiced eye inventoried the lavish nightclub; ran over the closely packed tables on the main floor, the tiers of tables on the mezzanine. Everything seemed to be going on as usual... until about eleven-thirty. Then he saw Franklin Penney ushered in and escorted to a table.

Franklin Penney! Wentworth's nerves tingled. Now he knew that his hunch was right; and fifteen minutes later he had additional confirmation. In the midst of a dance number he glimpsed Jigger Monahan leading two companions to a table that commanded every part of the big room. Jigger Monahan with two of his killers! Now there was no doubt about trouble brewing!

At the first opportunity Wentworth drew Tex Baker aside and warned him that an outbreak of some sort might occur. Baker nodded quick understanding and passed the word to the rest of his men. But it was not until the floor-show was at its height that the trouble started.

The club was dimly lighted, the spots turned on the score of girls who were tap-dancing in the center of the floor... when suddenly there was a fracas at the door. Loud voices and the sounds of a scuffle, of smacking fists and falling bodies. A moment later men appeared at the side exits, and others cut off escape by way of the stage entrance—hoodlums who covered the frightened guests with threatening automatics. Hoodlums who Wentworth recognized as Jigger Monahan's thugs.

"Keep your seats, everybody!" the voice of Blackie Leahy snarled an order as the music stopped. "This is a stick-up! Keep your seats—and nobody will get hurt!"

Now the thugs were advancing between the rows of tables, grabbing for wallets, snatching at jewels, systematically robbing the guests and dropping the loot into the same canvas sacks that had done duty in the subway. New Yorkers had learned not to attempt resistance to outrages of this sort. Helplessly they yielded their valuables and fervently hoped that nobody would make the overt move that would precipitate bloodshed.

Grimly Wentworth watched that well organized hold-up. There was nothing that he could do to prevent it. Even in the Spider's garb he would have no chance against these mobsters; would be shot down before he could do more than start the trouble that might result in a bloody massacre. It was better to wait and watch for an opportunity....

Then the decision was taken out of his hands. The management must have succeeded in notifying the police. The wail of sirens sounded outside on the street, the pound of feet charging across the foyer—and now the rear of the club was filled with blue uniforms. Policemen came running down the aisles, guns drawn—only to hesitate, then topple to the floor before they could pull a trigger!

Those policemen died like poison-blighted flies as the Green Death clutched at their throats, strangled them; and their appalling fate exploded the panic Wentworth had feared.

Screaming hysterically, women sprang to their feet—only to be knocked back into their chairs by the gunmen's fists. Forgetting their own danger, men leaped forward to defend their ladies—and the down-swinging gun barrels sent them sprawling over the toppling tables. In a moment the big room was echoing with the crash of glass, splintering of chairs, terrified screams of the quailing victims. Then the guns began to bark....

Now the lights had snapped on again. They only served to illuminate the pandemonium and betray those who were trying to slip out of the death-trap. Screaming frantically, the girls of the floor-show broke their routine and rushed toward the dressing rooms. After them, the orchestra members leaped to their feet and started down from their rostrum. Then, instead of fleeing, they charged forward behind Casimir Belotti.

Tex Baker had made good use of Wentworth's warning. In the rear of the stage and in the kitchen he had gathered a collection of clubs and knives. These had been smuggled out to the rostrum and distributed on the floor where they could readily be grabbed. Now, with a heavy sharpening steel in his hand, Baker ran close at Wentworth's heels. Before the surprised thugs knew what had happened, that charge from the rear was upon them.

"Get their guns," Wentworth had directed; and the musicians were swift to follow his order.

IN A few moments half a dozen of the gangsters were down—their guns were snatched up as quickly as they dropped from limp hands. From behind pillars and over-turned tables the embattled musicians exchanged shots with the thugs. Now some of the terrified customers were rallying to their aid. Confronted with opposition they had not expected, the hold-up men broke and retreated—fled in panic as Wentworth came arrowing through them with deadly accurate guns blazing.

Straight through them he darted, his objective the table where Jigger Monahan had arisen and was snarling orders at his panicky underlings. Deliberately Monahan raised his automatic and fired at Wentworth. But his on-coming target suddenly swerved out of the way. Like an eel Wentworth twisted to one side, flung himself beneath a table—then came up with a chair that sailed straight at Monahan's head.

The gangster tried to duck, but the chair caught him on the shoulder, spun him around. Before he could recover his balance, trigger another shot, Wentworth was almost upon him. Monahan's eyes blazed murderously. Twice he worked that speedy trigger finger that had won him his Underworld patronymic. But his aim was unsteady and at a difficult angle. His bullets missed their mark by a fraction of an inch—and the leaden slug that came at him did *not*. No more than six feet away from him Wentworth fired. The bullet buried itself in Trigger Monahan's cold-blooded heart....

Swiftly Wentworth bent over the fallen gang chief, and the bottom of his cigarette lighter pressed down on the center of Monahan's forehead—to leave there the crimson imprint of the Spider. He knew that this was not the Master of the Green Death—but Monahan had been one of the arch-criminal's most dependable tools. And once more the Spider had served notice that he made no truce, even though he knew that Nita was in the fiend's hands....

Wentworth pressed down on the lighter—and even before its mark was imprinted, his ears rang with a wild outburst of screaming. That terrified clamor came from behind the stage—from the dressing-rooms of the entertainers, girls whom it would not be worthwhile to rob.

Those girls....

Leaping away from Monahan's body, Wentworth dived through the struggling mob that blocked the aisles and tumbled over the up-set tables. He raced across the dance floor and into the stage entrance—to be slammed back roughly against the wall by a burly policeman at once. Now he saw that more policemen had arrived; saw that they were herding the frightened, protesting girls into waiting automobiles.

Policemen... but there was a difference. These policemen were not dying like the others. They seemed to be immune to the Green Death that was striking down their fellows....

The dressing-rooms were cleared in a few moments, and some of the newly arrived police strode into the battle-wrecked dining and dancing room. Wentworth saw them edge into the fray—saw, too, that they took little part in it. It was the women they were after—the good-looking young women, whom they extricated from the fracas and led back to the stage door.

The club had now become a veritable shambles. Hardly a table remained upright, and the floor was littered with bodies. Men and women groveled on their knees, desperately seeking a place of safety. Most of the tables had gone over, but as he came back through the stage door Wentworth saw one that was still standing. Franklin Penney suddenly leaped to his feet and backed away from it as if he expected to see it explode....

Franklin Penney... It was more than mere coincidence that the attorney was here in the Metropolitan when Jigger Monahan's hoodlums broke loose. Penney had expected something to happen; Wentworth had read that in his alert attitude, questing eyes.

Now he was making for a side door that was momentarily unguarded, and Wentworth followed. But as he reached the table from which Penney had just arisen he stopped and stared in amazement. There on the table a partly outspread napkin had been flung—a napkin with a rough drawing of a clutching green hand stamped upon it!

The mark of the Green Death! No wonder Penney had fled in terror!

Now the attorney was gone, but Wentworth ran to the side door in swift pursuit—and there almost collided with Jim Mack, the, detective! Head on, they met in the doorway, stared into each other's eyes.

"Just a minute, Casimir," Mack tried to stop him, as he reached out to grasp Wentworth's coat.

Jim Mack there in that blood-spattered dine-and-dance place... Why? Was that just accidental—or was he still following his dogged pursuit of the Spider? Still trying to prove that the Spider and the Master of the Green Death were one?

Wentworth did not wait to investigate. Without a word he hunched his shoulders and went through the doorway like a charging halfback, sending Mack spinning out of his way. Then he was out on the street—just in time to see the cars, loaded with the entertainers, swinging away from in front of the club. He leaped into a taxicab and, at gunpoint, forced the driver to fall in behind them.

CHAPTER 10
CRUISE TO HELL

IT TOOK Wentworth only a few moments to discover that the Metropolitan Casino was not the only night-club which had been raided. All Broadway was in an uproar, even worse than on the night of the motion-picture theater raids. Stricken policemen littered the streets everywhere. Yet police-guarded automobiles and patrol wagons, filled with girls, swept past without paying them the slightest attention!

A wild, riotous night such as the Great White Way had never seen! Pillaging mobs roamed the brightly lighted streets, sacking and looting on every side. Store windows were smashed, bars seized and turned into free-drink dispensaries, theaters desperately barricaded against the swarming hoodlums. Wherever Wentworth looked, panic-stricken spectators were fleeing, desperately anxious to get out of that gay play-district which suddenly had become a place of riotous terror. After them came the hoodlums... and after the hoodlums came the flames that leaped up where drink-crazed incendiaries had started fires!

"You're not being stuck up," Wentworth assured his trembling driver, as he holstered the threatening automatic. "Hang onto that car in front of you, and you'll rate a five-spot bonus."

The cabbie stuck to his quarry like a leech, after that—though Wentworth soon decided that it would make little difference if he lost the car immediately ahead. Now there were dozens of cars, all seemingly headed in the same direction. Police patrols, private cars, taxis, closed trucks—all heading west, toward the Hudson River docks.

There they converged on a pier that seemed to be doing a phenomenal business. A pier heavily guarded by policemen who kept the cars running up to the entrance and discharging their passengers in a steady stream. Wentworth paid off his driver a block beyond the pier and went back to it on foot. As he approached, a miasma of evil seemed to exude from the place, encompass him....

To a casual observer that busy scene might have passed as the usual sailing of a great trans-Atlantic liner. But this was different—terribly different. Here there was no laughing and joking, no hilarious merriment; these pier arrivals were screaming and sobbing, wildly begging to be released. Here there were no friends to give them a hearty send-off—only watchful policemen to seize them and rush them through the gates when they tried to break away from their escorts. This was more like a load of convicts about to be deported on a prison ship....

Wentworth mingled with the crowding cars and got close enough to the open gateway so that he could see out onto the pier, where a rusty-looking freighter was tied up.

Gangways from the discolored hull were down fore and aft—and up them were being dragged two streams of tearful, vainly struggling girls. Hundreds of them, scantily clad night-club performers and evening-gowned guests who had been snatched from their places at the tables. All were being herded up those gangways to where dark-skinned men stood on the decks waiting to receive them. Men who lashed out at them savagely with leather whips, to hurry them down into the open hatches—cutting into their backs and tearing screams from their lips!

That shabby hulk was a slave-ship. A vile floating prison into which the unfortunate girls were being driven like a herd of cattle. A slave-ship more horrible than any that ever sailed the seas—loaded not with laborers but with helpless women who would be transported and sold to the infamous bordellos of Latin America! A white-slave ship being loaded under the protection of the New York police!

Wentworth stared at several of those policemen—and the reason for their strange immunity to the Green Death was clear to him. One of them, who passed just inside the gate, was Monte Pelano! They were gangsters, killers masquerading in police uniforms!

FOR MORE than two blocks farther uptown, the piers presented a solid, unbroken front to the street. But beyond that was another eight-foot fence with a gateway closing off the automobile entrance. The pier was dark, but Wentworth could make out the shapes of two summer vacation steamers, their season finished, tied up beside it. At least this would give him a chance to reach the water.

The white front of his evening shirt was a sorry mess by the time he had scaled the fence. Still, it stood out like a headlight in the darkness. With his coat lapels turned up and pinned around

For a minute he held the body as a shield—then let it fall to the deck!

his throat, he started down the dark pier—and barely escaped the watchman who came to investigate the creaking of the fence as he went over the top.

Once the watchman was past, Wentworth sped swiftly beneath the open shed of the pier. Beyond the summer steamers a tug was moored—and from its stern floated exactly what he needed. A skiff!

Silently Wentworth lowered himself into it, cast loose. He headed downstream, keeping close to the piers.

He drifted up against the hull and held the skiff off until he reached a point beneath the bow, where the flukes of the anchor, projecting through the anchor-chain port, extended out over the side of the ship. From beneath his shirt he quickly uncoiled the thin silken rope that was wound loosely around his body. Three times he cast upward with it before it settled over the anchor.

Hand over hand, he climbed to the deck and then over the side, when he saw that the way was clear. The excitement was all on the pier side of the vessel; nobody was paying any attention to the starboard side. It gave him an opportunity to creep back until he reached the fore-deck ladder and descended to the deck below. Then he dived beneath the ladder, slipped into the dark forecastle.

There he sat down on a bunk and took quick stock. He was aboard the *La Conga*, of Buenos Aires—no doubt bound for that Argentine city unless he could prevent the vessel from leaving the harbor. That was an impossible undertaking while they were at the pier, and the crew would be augmented by the gangsters on the shore. His only chance to seize the vessel would be after it cast off—then he would be one man against there was no telling how many. One man in evening clothes, spotted the moment he dared to step out on deck!

That must be remedied at once. Quickly his pencil-flash darted around the forecastle, picked out an array of clothing pegged beside the berths. A pair of heavy, grease-smeared trousers that would slip on over those he wore; a weather-stained pull-over sweater of uncertain color; a dirty cap with a broken visor. Now he was ready to investigate the *La Conga*.

The girls were still being dragged aboard when he stepped out of the forecastle and stole along the starboard side toward the center of the ship. Now he saw that the stream of victims was almost ended. Sailors were fastening the aft hatch-covers in place—a curious hatch cover that was provided with a trap in the top so that the human cargo below could be fed and aired!

The *La Conga* was ready to sail—and to Wentworth's dismay he saw that the police-masquerading thugs were going to sail with her! More than thirty of them tramped up the gangways and went to the deckhouse that evidently was to be their quarters. At least thirty armed thugs to be added to the *La Conga's* crew!

If anyone could gain command of this hell-ship and force it to disgorge its miserable cargo, it was the Spider. Yet, as he contemplated the task before him, Wentworth realized that never had he faced odds so overwhelming.

EVEN AS he stood there, momentarily halted by the realization of what he faced, disaster swooped down upon him.

Suddenly a gruff voice accosted him out of the gloom, and a sailor strode forward.

"Thief!" the sailor roared in Spanish. "Now you are so bold that you wear my clothes right out on deck! It is not enough that you steal my things; now you show me that you have them! But perhaps I can show you a new way to remove a stolen sweater!"

Out of his belt he pulled a long knife that glinted wickedly as a ray of light fell upon it. With a snarl of rage he came charging forward—and in that split second Wentworth's thoughts machine-gunned through his mind. He did not dare shoot the fellow, for fear of bringing the others down upon him. He did not dare come to grips with him for fear the fellow might yell for help. Flight was his only hope… flight to the forecastle.

Just in time he darted under the down-swinging knife, started forward. His pursuer was close behind. Wentworth reached the forecastle, dashed inside—and the moment his man opened the door to follow he was yanked inside and borne to the floor. Desperately they locked each other in grips of iron; held on with one arm while the other flailed away.

The sailor was big, strong—tougher than Wentworth had feared. He was so big that it was almost impossible to get a wrestling grip on him; so strong that the pressure of his constricting arm threatened to break Wentworth's ribs. Grimly, silently they pitched, rolled. The sailor had lost his knife in the struggle, but Wentworth was unable to get at his guns.

Back, as far as possible out of reach, he held his head—and at that moment caught the sound of approaching feet. Sailors were coming to the forecastle! In a moment he would be overwhelmed, dragged outside to the gangsters—and identified....

Sheer desperation brought Wentworth's head smashing forward like a downs winging club. Straight into the sailor's snapping teeth he smashed; again and again, until his forehead was cut and blood ran down into his face. But the fellow gasped—his hold broke. In the next instant Wentworth's fists smashed into his face with a pile-driving one-two that knocked him out.

Swiftly Wentworth flashed on his light. There, at the head of the forecastle, was a closet, a locker of some sort. It would have to do. Seizing the sailor by his collar, he dragged him to the door, opened it and shoved the inert body in among a mass of tarpaulin and miscellaneous ship's supplies. Then he dived in after it, closing the door just as the sailors came tramping into the forecastle.

For a moment Wentworth tensed, fearful that they had seen the locker door close. But they slumped down on their bunks, and he realized that he had gained a reprieve. He went to work rapidly with his make-up kit. His skillful fingers worked blindly in the dark, creating the Spider's ugly visage. From inside the lining of his tuxedo came the black cape and floppy brimmed hat. The Spider was ready....

He stooped, grabbed up the unconscious body at his feet. Then slowly he opened the door—stood revealed there, a fantastic demon who covered the dozen sailors in the forecastle with a leveled automatic.

"The devil!" A Cuban crossed himself frantically. "See—he has killed Big Juan, who could out-fight any two men!"

"No, not the devil," Wentworth answered in their own tongue. He let the unconscious body drop to the floor, advanced upon them. "Men call me the Spider. But my sting is not for those who do not interfere with me. You—" he indicated two of them—"get ropes out of that locker and tie up these others. Tie their wrists, ankles—and mouths."

Swiftly he was obeyed. He completed the job by trussing up the two who remained… Now a dozen of the crew were temporarily incapacitated. Wentworth relieved them of half a dozen knives. Then he turned out the light and left them in darkness, cat-footing his way toward mid-ship.

The vessel had left the pier, slipped out into the river and reached the Upper Bay. Now it was gathering speed, and minutes were becoming infinitely precious.

AT THE foot of the deck superstructure, Wentworth hesitated, listening to the voices that came down from above. There were three stories to this deckhouse. The first seemed to be taken up with store-rooms and kitchens; the second with staterooms; the third, just beneath the captain's quarters and the bridge, was the combination dining-room and salon. It was from there that the hum of voices came.

Noiselessly Wentworth went up the steps. He crouched in the doorway, momentarily unseen by the thugs who had gathered around three tables, playing cards and shooting dice. It was a dicer, reaching for one of the cubes that had fallen to the floor, who first saw him. But before the fellow could do more than gape, Wentworth's guns roared in a tattoo that shattered the lights, plunging the little salon into darkness.

"The Spider!" a man yelled. His warning completed the panic.

Just inside the doorway Wentworth crouched, automatics gripped. Almost wherever he shot in that close-packed room, he was certain to hit a foe. It was like shooting down trapped beasts. But when he thought of those poor girls huddled miserably in the hold and remembered the fate to which these thugs were ready to consign them, his heart hardened.

Now more than a dozen guns were blazing at him, turning the salon into a crashing shooting gallery. The thugs fired at the flashes of his weapons. But the Spider was like quicksilver. He seemed to be all over the salon at once—firing at their own gun flashes.

That fight was short-lived. Thugs threw themselves to the floor, crept to the doorway; ran a gauntlet of lead to drag themselves over the steps and go crawling and tumbling down the companionway. Soon the last of them had scurried off into the darkness. When Wentworth flashed on his light, it revealed nine bodies sprawled on the floor—corpses or men wholly without fight.

He relieved them of their guns, crammed them into his pockets. He opened one of the salon windows, climbed out—lowering himself down the face of the superstructure floor by floor. By now there was a great hullabaloo on deck. Men were racing toward the deckhouse with lanterns and guns—surrounding it as they crept up on the dining-salon. But now the Spider was hovering over the trapdoor in the top of the aft hatch.

As soon as he opened that trap, a groan of utter misery rose up from hundreds of throats. His penetrating cackle of warning silenced them. Swiftly he tied the rope, taken with him from the anchor flukes, to the trap. He let himself down into the stygian hold that was jammed with helpless women.

The air in the great, barn-like hold was becoming heavy. His flash revealed the reason. Crude bunks, six high, had been erected here, one tier beside the other, so close together that there was hardly room to move between them. Even these were not nearly adequate to accommodate the number of captives. Women were lying on the floor, packed tightly against one another, sobbing their misery into one another's arms—hundreds of them!

For an instant he turned the beam of the flash on his own face. A low gasp of horror rose from the captives.

"The Spider!" they moaned—but now the name that so many people hated and dreaded was like a prayer on their lips.

"Yes, the Spider," he gritted acknowledgment. "The Spider come to help those who help themselves. You know where this ship is bound—to South America. You know what awaits you there… You have one chance to escape that fate—by following me. If you do that, you will either win your freedom or you will die!"

"That's all I ask." A tight-lipped, haggard-eyed young woman came to his side. "Anything would be better than this—and the *other*. What do you want us to do, Spider?"

From his pockets the Spider disgorged fourteen automatics and revolvers, spoils of his battle in the salon. These he spread out on a bunk.

"I want fourteen of you to pick up those guns and follow me." His glittering eyes surveyed them challengingly. "Fourteen who are not afraid to shoot to kill—or be killed."

The guns were snatched up so fast that he hardly saw them go. Dozens insisted upon fighting with their bare hands! Wentworth's heart leaped with satisfaction.

Up the rope he climbed and through the trap, to stand there helping the girls as they came up to him. Nearly fifty of them were out of the hold before he called a halt, fearful that more than that number might only hinder the clash with the gangsters.

MEN'S VOICES were calling back and forth in English and Spanish from the superstructure. Now new bulbs were being screwed into the salon lighting fixtures. The windows glowed again. But a snarl of disappointed rage came from the gangsters when they found only their dead and badly wounded companions in the bullet-scarred room.

"What did you expect, you fools?" a familiar sounding voice rasped at them. "Think he would stay here and wait for you to come back for him? He's down there on deck somewhere. By hell—I'll bet he is meddling with the women! Get down to the hatches!"

But when they arrived, the Spider and his allies were waiting. In the darkness that surrounded the entrances to the deckhouse they crouched, fingers on triggers, barely restraining their impatience. Not until he gave the word, would they fire. The gangsters were down on the deck level, swarming out into the darkness, before the guns opened up… and then they were mowed down before they could even flee.

Panic-stricken yells warned those above what awaited them—but a raging voice urged them on. Down they came charging into the stabbing gunfire and broke through it by sheer desperation. Wentworth heard them go racing across the decks, he knew that now his position was bad. Now the men would return with reinforcements from the deck staff and the black gang down in the boiler room. His desperate little band would be overwhelmed, unless….

"Up the stairs!" he ordered, and led the way with blasting guns that cleared the entrance to the superstructure. Now they must fight!

On the second landing he halted them, ranged them around the companionway. They must hold it against an assault from below. With four armed girls at his back, he went up the next flight to the disordered salon. It was deserted… but all the surviving gangsters could not have broken through his cordon. There were others… on the floor above.

Crouching low, an almost indistinguishable smudge in the darkness, the Spider went up the companionway to the captain's quarters and the bridge. Behind him came four desperate, grim-faced girls who had just stepped out of New York's most torrid night-club revues.

All was quiet up here on the highest level. Lights gleamed in the captain's rooms, but the curtains were drawn. Wentworth reached the door, grasped the knob—and suddenly thrust inward as he leaped back into the darkness. One of the bullets, blasting out from the interior, caught him in the left shoulder. He reeled against the railing at the edge of the narrow deck—but only for a moment. Then he was back at the cabin wall. Now the advantage was his; it was light in that cabin, dark outside.

The Spider glided to one of the windows and his automatics roared through the pane. Four killers were in the cabin, but they were doomed before they could switch off the lights. Wentworth's guns accounted for two of them, and the other pair went down under the fire that poured in from the other shattered windows.

At the head of his girl allies the Spider sprang into the death-strewn cabin. Four dead thugs... but none was the man he wanted. Who was that man? The Master of the Green Death? Wentworth did not know... but he knew that there must be someone of superior caliber to these dumb gun-hands!

At the far end of the cabin was another door. Another trap? Warily, the Spider approached—then was swept off his feet by two thugs who abruptly leaped out. Vainly he triggered his guns. One was empty; the other clicked impotently after a single shot. Using them as clubs, he swung at his attackers. One of the automatics was wrested from his hand. The other smashed up into the face of the assailant kneeling on top of him, sent him reeling. The Spider sprang to his feet.

Terrified, his other opponent attempted to flee but ran straight into the arms of the infuriated girls. Wentworth did not stop to see the fellow's end. He dived through the doorway into the cabin beyond, heard the door click shut behind. For an instant the cabin seemed to be empty. Then, at last, he saw the man he sought.

From behind a curtain, that served as a makeshift closet, stepped Franklin Penney. An automatic was leveled in his fist, a look of devilish satisfaction on his face.

"Thanks for your assistance, Spider," he sneered. "That will make a few less to payoff out of the profits of this expedition."

Inexorably he came forward, evidently aware that the Spider's gun was empty. Step by step… cunning purpose in his eyes. He intended to take the Spider alive, torture him—perhaps eventually to hand him over to his killers to exact full vengeance for the death of their mates. Death from the muzzle of a gun would be too easy for the Spider….

Wentworth watched him come; waited his chance. Suddenly he hurled his useless gun. Penney had been expecting that. He ducked and the weapon sailed harmlessly over his shoulder. Grinning evilly, he came on… and the Spider was helpless. Then into his mind flashed a memory of that green hand on the napkin on Penney's table in the Metropolitan Casino!

It was a chance—a wild, almost hopeless chance. But it might work if that hand possessed the significance he believed….

Acting on that desperate hunch, he suddenly sprang toward Penney. The fingers of his right hand outstretched clutchingly in reproduction of that crude drawing… and the effect was astounding. Franklin Penney stared at those constricting fingers, his eyes widening. It was as if he felt them closing around his throat! For a moment he stood there transfixed.

In that instant the Spider reached him—seized the threatening gun barrel and twisted it so that its bullets smashed harmlessly into the cabin wall.

As they struggled for possession of the gun, an eerie transformation came over the attorney. His face began to change color, acquire a greenish tinge! Terror flared in his eyes, his features twisted in agony... and were distorted horribly as he dropped to the floor, threshing there until he died, a victim of the Green Death!

UTTERLY NONPLUSSED by this miracle he had wrought Wentworth stared down at the twitching body. He had not killed Penney. The Master of the Green Death had fulfilled that napkin warning—but how? How could a man be stricken down with no Green Death Master near him; with no mark but that ghastly greenish color upon him? It was almost as if Wentworth's clutching hand, alone, had frightened Franklin Penney to death....

Suddenly daylight seemed to dawn outside. A searchlight from near the stern had been turned on the superstructure, to light it brightly for the benefit of the gangsters and crew members now closing in on it. A renewed burst of firing broke out below. Wentworth realized that the girls were being hard pressed, slowly but steadily driven back from the companionway.

The glaring searchlight meant that he would be clearly revealed when he left the cabin. But already Wentworth's speeding brain had evolved a way to transform that danger into an advantage. Holding Franklin Penney's body as a shield, he stepped out on deck. He lifted it to the rail so that all below would be sure to recognize it—then let it fall to the deck. He leaped back, raced to the companionway joining his allies with the additional guns collected from the fallen thugs in the cabin.

The death of their leader had an immediate effect on the gangsters. Shouts of dismay went up from them, and again the fearsome name of the Spider echoed over the vessel. Wentworth wasted not a moment. Quick to take advantage of their momentary demoralization, he led his girls in a charge that drove the thugs back and routed the panicky crew....

Relentlessly the Spider pressed them, his reloaded guns cutting them down mercilessly. Now he found that he had an unexpected ally. Just as two desperate thugs leaped at him from a lifeboat concealment, a blue-coated figure closed with them, savagely.

Jim Mack! The detective evidently had gotten aboard the ship in the same police disguise the crooks had used! Without a word, he took his place at Wentworth's side and added the bark of his guns to the roar of Wentworth's automatics—Jim Mack fighting beside the Spider, the arch-criminal he was sworn to capture!

The beaten thugs were driven to the stern of the ship. Then Wentworth turned to continue the cleanup sweep to the bow— and to the bridge, where the officers were making every effort to get out to sea. By now the ship was leaving the Upper Bay, starting through the Narrows and heading for the open water.

"Good work!" the Spider's harsh voice rasped to his silent ally. "Stay with the girls. I'll wireless for help."

Before Mack could answer, he slipped away in the darkness and reached the little radio shack near the stern. His guns sent the trembling operator cowering into a corner. Quickly Wentworth took over the set, began calling for aid. He had little hope of assistance from the police. But within a few minutes he had contacted the coast guard and explained conditions aboard the *La Conga*. He was assured that aid would be rushed immediately.

By the time he returned to the deck the sound of firing had almost ceased. Jim Mack was in control of the deck. He had driven the gangsters into the forecastle with the crew, posting girls at the companionways so that no aid could come up from below. How long they would be able to hold that advantage was problematical....

But in a few minutes the lights of two coast guard cutters became visible, speeding toward the vessel. Now searchlights focused upon it, making it a plain target for their uncovered guns.

THE SPIDER'S work there was finished. Silently he stole to a portion of the vessel that was in darkness and there divested himself of his hat and cape. He put them away securely in the oiled-silk container in the lining of his coat. Quickly his fingers went to work on his face, stripping off the Spider's make-up and restoring the countenance of Casimir Belotti—his only protection in the event police picked him up.

Quietly he lowered himself over the side. He cut the water in a clean, noiseless dive, and started toward the Staten Island shore. With strong, easy strokes he glided through the water; and as he swam a steady current of thoughts sped through his puzzled mind.

Franklin Penney was dead... and it was Penney's crooked brain that had conceived the *La Conga's* monstrous raid. But he knew that in Penney he had *not* conquered the Master of the Green Death.

Penney had been no more than another underling; a pariah who had tried to use the Machiavellian fiend as a cover.

But who could the master-criminal be? Professor Thrall? That seemed most likely; seem almost proved… and yet Wentworth found it hard to believe even the evidence of his own eyes. If not Thrall….

Suddenly the face of Jim Mack flashed into his mind—and with it a question. What did he really know about Mack? The man professed to be a detective and had appeared several times with the police. But might it not be possible that his anxiety to corner the Spider and pin the Green Death guilt upon him was dictated by a motive of self-protection? Might it not be possible that Jim Mack was the Master of the Green Death—or at least one of the fiend's agents?

The wound in Wentworth's shoulder had sapped his strength far more than he had realized. Now, as he drew himself up among the pilings beneath a dock, he was very weary. With difficulty he started to climb out of the water—when suddenly a hand reached out, grabbed him.

Astounded, he whirled. In the darkness he could just make out a face that seemed to have sprung right from his thoughts— the face of Jim Mack, who had tenaciously followed him from the slave-ship!

CHAPTER 11
THE GREEN DEATH

WHEN JIM MACK realized Wentworth's weakness, he quickly pulled himself up under the dock and lowered a hand to his companion. Solicitously he lifted Wentworth and helped him to a stringer to which the piles were attached—insisted that he rest while his wounded shoulder was being examined and dressed. When that was finished Mack eyed him silently and uncomfortably.

"I don't like what I've got to do any more than you will like it, Casimir," he said regretfully. "But duty is duty—that's that. You thought I was wasting my time trailing the Spider. But I've learned a lot since the night I told you about that. For one thing, I've learned that you and Blinky McQuade are the same person—and that you both are the Spider! Following you ashore here tonight just clinches what I knew already. But it puts it up to me to take you to headquarters—no matter what I might think about it personally."

Wentworth eyed the Irish face sharply. Now there was no doubt of Jim Mack's genuineness—no doubt that he would do exactly as he said he would. It meant arrest and exposure for Wentworth; meant pinning the Spider personality onto him and railroading him to the electric chair—while the Green Death was left free to ravage the city. And that meant leaving Nita helpless in the inhuman monster's hands....

Even as those thoughts flashed through his mind, Wentworth realized his overpowering weakness. He must have lost far more

165

blood than he had thought. Now his head swam, and he feared that dizziness would overwhelm him. Obviously he was in no condition to risk a physical encounter with the husky detective. But if he could get the drop....

"No, you don't, Spider!" Mack's automatic covered him unerringly. "I know your speed on the draw, but I can plug you before you get a gun clear. Steady now," he came closer. "I'm going to relieve you of those guns—and I won't kill you, unless you make me do it."

He snatched the automatics from their shoulder holsters, and Wentworth was entirely at his mercy. Docilely he went with Mack—out from under the dock to the street, where the detective hailed a cab and commandeered it for a trip to police headquarters in Manhattan.

On the way Jim Mack's conscience seemed to trouble him.

"You're not a bad egg—sometimes, Spider," he said thoughtfully. "You did a mighty good job out there on the boat. You pulled my bacon out of the fire a couple of times. Don't think I don't appreciate that. Thinking about it makes taking you in seem pretty rotten. But what in hell can I do? Answer that yourself."

"First, you might be quite certain that I am this Blinky McQuade person you talk about—and that I am the Spider," Wentworth said quietly. "Has it occurred to you that I may have been on the *La Conga* as innocently as you; that I may have been trying to help those poor girls the same as you—and the Spider?"

"Let's skip the boat, Casimir," Mack dismissed that objection. "I've got so much on you I don't need that. That night in the fur warehouse—I wasn't 'out' as completely as you thought I was. I had spells of semi-consciousness, and I saw you getting out of your Spider makeup. But I couldn't prove anything on you then; and, hell, you saved my life down there. But I kept on your track after that. I followed every possible lead, checked up on everything you did. I got plenty on you."

Incident after incident Mack mentioned as he seemed to be trying to justify himself. As he listened, Wentworth realized that Mack had appeared so frequently on his trail simply because of the dogged perseverance with which he kept at his task. A patient plodder, he had spared no pains to build up proof for what he believed.

"Duty or no duty, I'd be tempted to close my eyes and let the Spider take a walk—if it wasn't for this Green Death business," he finished his self vindication. "That's raw, Casimir. That wipes out everything decent the Spider ever did!"

"If you are so certain that I am the Spider, and that the Spider is the one responsible for this Green Death, how do you account for the note I sent you to warn you about the subway hold-ups?" Wentworth tried once more to sway him. "Here—" he took a pencil and paper from his pocket and rewrote part of the note, "this is my handwriting. The same that was on the note, is it not? Does it seem common sense to you that I would warn you so that you would be able to block my men if I were operating this Green Death? Doesn't that note prove that I was *fighting* the gangsters instead of working with them?"

"No, it don't," Mack answered flatly. "That proves definitely that you're the Spider. It was the Spider who broke up the hold-up near the Fulton Street station, we know that. One train hold-up out of more than a hundred! That was swell alibi stuff for you—but it's not good enough. I covered every angle of that, Casimir—even dug up Deuce Behrman and made him talk. Everything I uncovered makes you the Spider."

There was no gainsaying the man, Wentworth realized. Jim Mack had a one-track mind, but a grimly thorough one. He was not brilliant, but his dogged plodding was more dangerous than brilliance. Now it had succeeded in doing what hundreds of far superior detectives had never been able to accomplish. He had the Spider helpless and under arrest and was in a fair way to prove his case once they reached headquarters....

IT WAS nearly one-thirty when they reached headquarters, and the building was deserted except for the regular precinct force. Mack led his prisoner past the desk and into the back room, where the reserves who were not asleep were engaged in a poker game. Seven of them were holding cards, while several others sat by and watched. They gave Wentworth no more than a passing glance when Mack sat him down in a chair at one side of the room. But every eye turned in his direction when they heard the detective call up Sanford Dane and the district attorney—and announce that he had captured the Spider!

The Spider—a prisoner here in headquarters!

Curiously they stared at him—and Wentworth fully expected to be recognized in his own guise at any moment. Only his haggard and bedraggled appearance, he was convinced, enabled his disguise to stand up under that searching scrutiny. Again dizzy weakness assailed him. The room began to swim before his eyes, and he was on the verge of fainting when one of the policemen realized his condition and poured him a glass of water from a pitcher which stood at one side of the card table.

"Maybe you're right, Mack," the cop shrugged, as he brought back the emptied glass and poured a drink for himself, "but this guy's not much like my idea of the Spider. You better be right, boy, if you bring Sanford Dane running down here at this time of night!"

With that the players returned to their cards and the kibitzers to their watching of the hands. His escape from recognition so far had been providential, Wentworth told himself. But when Sanford Dane and the district attorney arrived his good luck was destined to end. Once they were there he would be cross-questioned and brow-beaten, examined with eagle eyes. Even if he managed to pass that ordeal, he would be booked and locked up—would be searched and forced to bathe! That would be the end of his make-up and would no doubt divulge the Spider's raiment and accoutrement hidden in his clothing....

Once more he considered the advisability of making a desperate break for freedom. If he could spring across the room and grab one of those holstered revolvers hanging from belts over the backs of the chairs in which the players sat....

Before he could set himself for such an attempt, things began to happen swiftly. In the hallway he heard footsteps, Sanford Dane's sonorous voice—and at the same moment an argument arose among the card-players. A mild argument at first, it had now become bitter.

"There's my discards—two of them!" a red-faced patrolman shouted. He pointed to two cards in the center of the table. "That's what I called for—two cards. I can't help it if you gimme three. Take the last one back—I don't want it. You got another guess coming if you think I'm gonna chuck away a hand like this!"

"Rules are rules," another player insisted heatedly. "I don't give a damn about the size of the pot—you've got six cards, so your hand's dead. That's the rule, and that's the way we play here."

"You don't care about the size of the pot!" the red-faced man raged. "You got nearly all the chips in front of you now—and this time I suppose you've got another of those sneaker hands. Well, I don't give a—"

He had half-risen from his chair, when suddenly he froze in his half-crouch and grasped his throat. A low moan escaped from his distended lips—and a greenish tinge began to spread over his face! Before his mates could grab him he toppled over on the table and rolled to the floor. There he writhed convulsively as the ghastly death color deepened!

First this man… then the one with whom he had argued! In less than half a minute they were both stricken, stretched on the floor. When Sanford Dane grasped the situation and ran to kneel beside them, they were dead—victims of the Green Death!

THE GREEN DEATH there in police headquarters! Wentworth stared at the still bodies, at the disordered card table, the places where the dead men had sat, at the empty glasses beside their stacks of chips—but found no answer! There could be only one explanation for that swift tragedy. That explanation meant that he, too, was infected with the virus of the Green Death—was a potential victim of the dread scourge!

Whatever had caused those men to die had been in the water they had drunk! That, he reviewed swiftly, would apply in every case of the Green Death—would explain why some policemen fell victims to the scourge while others seemed impervious to it. Horeski had been stricken when he became excited, fear-stricken; Penney had succumbed when he started to struggle; the policemen, arriving at the scenes of crimes, had collapsed when they attempted to go into action.

That was it—excitement, action... Whatever drug it was that the water contained seemed to remain dormant as long as the victims did not exert themselves. Therefore, he apparently would be safe as long as he remained calm. Any excitement, any rush of physical activity, would doom him!

But to remain calm and cool, when his life hung on the question of whether or not Sanford Dane would recognize him... Could he do that?

In a flash the Green Death's scheme of operation came home to him. He remembered that blank-faced man who ran away from him after coming out of the office building on Twenty-eighth Street; remembered how the fellow had seemed to disappear into nowhere. And in that moment Wentworth knew that he must get out of headquarters without a second's delay....

The paralyzing horror that momentarily gripped everyone in that back room gave him the opportunity he needed. Taking advantage of their absorption, he stepped forward and quietly lifted a revolver from one of the policemen's holsters; another from the one that hung over the chair beside it. Before they realized what he was doing, both guns were covering them.

"Stand where you are," he commanded softly. "That means you, too, Dane," as the acting commissioner began to swell with rage and stalk forward majestically. "I will shoot you down, if necessary. But there is a much more effective killer than I present here at this moment. The Green Death is here, gentlemen. You just saw what it did to those men on the floor. It will do the same to you. You are all infected with it, all in its grip; and you will be stricken down the moment you get excited or try to put up a struggle of any sort. If you want to live, be calm, gentlemen; quiet and inactivity are your only hope for life! If any of you doubt that, test it—try a little exercise."

Stunned by the horror, those men stood like statues. None dared make the test by so much as a swift motion! Ashen-faced, they stared at him as if he were Death itself. Wentworth realized that they considered him the Green Death; believed that he had killed the card-players to demonstrate his power—and could kill the rest of them with equal ease.

Let them keep that idea for the present. There was no time for him to enlighten them. Their terror would serve him in good stead. Slowly he moved toward the door, and no man hindered his departure. But as soon as he was out of the room they would be at the telephone, attempting to have him intercepted.

Speed was essential now—but he could not speed! He must be slow, calm, quiet, take things easily. That was his ironical prescription for life, at a time when every moment was infinitely precious!

Prickles ran up and down his spine as he walked through the corridors and passed the man at the desk. Casually went down the broad steps and out onto the sidewalk. At any moment now they would be after him, closing in! Desperately he tried not to hurry—his every instinct being to run as fast as his legs would carry him. Even excitement might bring the Green Death. The Green Death or the police… It was a toss-up which would get him as he walked sedately toward the corner, trying his best not to realize that he was holding his muscles in check by sheer willpower….

Then a cruising taxicab picked him up. With a sigh of relief, he directed the driver to Lexington Avenue and Twenty-eighth Street and sank back on the seat… to mop away the perspiration that filmed his forehead!

Momentarily he expected to hear the wail of police sirens, but there was no sign of pursuit. At the corner of Twenty-eighth Street he paid off the driver, walked back to the charred doorway of the fire-gutted office building. From there he took his bearings and located the manhole through which the blank-faced man had vanished.

It was loose; came up readily when he thrust his fingers through the holes and lifted. Beneath it was a ladder that led down into the dark passageway below. Trying to make his movements slow and deliberate, he stepped down into the hole and pulled the cover in place above him. Now his flashlight speared into the darkness and revealed the maze of pipes and cables that lined the walls of the narrow passageway.

Which way should he go? Wentworth started in the direction of the corner and branched out into another tunnel that should run downtown, followed it until he reached another that should run beneath Twenty-seventh Street. Carefully he searched the thick dust on the floor. His light picked out what he sought—a faint trail in the dust that led toward the east. Slowly he followed it through several intercepting passageways until he was utterly lost in the subterranean maze. Then suddenly it brought him up against a heavy sheet-iron door. Now he halted, frowned.

Cautiously he tried the handle, but the door was locked—a simple, old-fashioned house lock that readily yielded to his skeleton keys. Slowly he opened the door, peered into a dark, silent basement room. It appeared to be empty, but the moment he stepped past the doorway the heavy door slammed shut behind him and a dim overhead light flashed on—to reveal the blank-faced men who crouched close against the wall, ready to leap upon him!

The blank-faced men and Stephen Thrall! This was their basement meeting-room—the room he had not been able to find when he searched the Thrall house from top to bottom!

Now Thrall stood at the far end of it, framed in another low doorway; stood there and smiled malignantly as the blank-faced men sprang upon Wentworth and bore him, unresisting, to the floor.

CHAPTER 12
A SPIDER'S END

WENTWORTH HAD half-realized where he was going—and yet had walked blindly into a trap for which he should have been prepared. Bitterly he condemned himself as the blank-faced men pinned him down, confiscating his revolvers. He had known that this subterranean route must connect up with Thrall's basement room, but had stumbled into it after unwittingly setting off an alarm that put the old man on guard.

The Professor realized this also—and seemed to enjoy Wentworth's chagrin. "So you enjoyed our company so much that you have returned for another visit, Mr. Wentworth?" he sneered. "Oh, my mistake—I am not supposed to know that you are Mr. Wentworth, am I? But you see I rather expected to have you dropping in on me ever since I took charge of Miss van Sloan. She could not resist the temptation to pry into my affairs."

He went on. "The last time you managed to escape. I hoped that would teach you a lesson. Now I see that you enjoy playing with death. But I am afraid you've tried your luck once too often. You have lost, Wentworth. You have so cleverly solved the secret of my subterranean entrance! No doubt you also have discovered how the Green Death is administered. Now I cannot possibly allow you to live."

The manholes... and the Green Death. Wentworth had suspected that there must be some tie-up between them. Now he was certain of it. It was through the manholes that the Green

Death was administered; through contact with the water pipes running into the homes of persons who were to be stricken. This explained how a whole precinct of policemen could be stricken by the Green Death while others at the same scene were not affected. The station-house water had been doctored where it left the mains to enter the building.

That was the secret Thrall knew Wentworth had uncovered with his finding of the underground entrance to this hideout. And for that discovery the penalty was death!

"There are several other troublesome persons of your sort whom I have been accumulating for some time," the Professor was saying. "Now is a good time to clean house. Tonight, my dear Wentworth, you will be my guest at a little farewell party."

As he finished, he turned to the doorway behind him, pressed his finger against a button concealed in one of the panels. The whole room seemed to change! Wentworth saw that the entire side wall was disappearing; was sinking into the floor to double the size of the room and open the way into what must have been the building next door!

There was a way of escape—if only he could reach it! Perfectly tranquil in the hands of the blank-faced men until that moment, Wentworth suddenly hurled himself forward and almost succeeded in gaining his freedom. All but two of them were taken by surprise. Those two were hanging on desperately. Wentworth's fist lashed out, caught one on the jaw; then he whirled on the other… and abruptly subsided like a pricked balloon.

The pain in his shoulder and dizzy spinning of his head had shouted a warning in his ear. The Green Death! It was while struggling like this that Franklin Penney had died! Wentworth could almost feel the ghastly green discoloration creeping up into his cheeks, as he dropped his arms and let the blank-faced men bear him to the floor. No doubt now but that his system had absorbed the poisoned atmosphere at the station-house.

Caution....

His return was the signal for departure. Held securely between two of the blank-faced retainers, Wentworth was led upstairs and through a corridor to the front door of the building. There he saw that a number of cars were waiting at the curb... and sensed something else that was somehow puzzling.

What...?

The hallway—that was it! It was decorated and furnished just as it had been the last time he passed through the building... yet it was somehow different. The exact change eluded him, but when he got outside and glanced back at the house his eyes widened in surprise. The building was just like its neighbors on either side—but it was not the Thrall house to which he and Hugo Schoenheit had brought the Hanley baby. That building was next door!

The building next door... Gradually the elusive pieces of this baffling murder puzzle were beginning to take shape and fall into place in his mind. But now it was too late; now he was utterly helpless....

UP SECOND AVENUE to the Queensborough Bridge that little cavalcade of cars sped; over the bridge and out to the Flushing Meadows, where the World's Fair, now closed down for the winter months, loomed in the darkness like a weird ghost town, a fantastic city of vast emptiness. A city of emptiness for all except Stephen Thrall—but he approached it confidently and seemed to know just what to expect. Not a soul appeared anywhere until his cars drew up in front of one of the automobile entrances and one sounded a short signal.

Promptly it was answered. The gates swung wide, and the cars rolled into a world that had been closed up and put away until the following year. Along empty streets they sped and turned into a parking-space behind one of the largest of the exhibition buildings—the great Hall of Machinery, Wentworth recognized it, as he was taken from the automobile and led to a side door.

From the outside that building was dark and as deserted looking as any of its neighbors, but when he reached the interior he found that there were lights—carefully guarded from without. Not the original bright illumination which millions of visitors had seen during the past months, but dim, subdued lighting that cast an eerie glow over the vast hall.

That strange glow made the large-scale models of various machines stand out like fantastic, half-human creatures; gave it the aspect of a supernatural world. Like a mad artist's conception of Hades, Wentworth thought—and only when he reached the end of the great hall did he realize how apt was that description.

Here a great working model of a new, many-bladed mowing-machine had been erected—a model nearly twenty feet high that had fascinated Fair visitors as its flashing blades moved around and around. Then those blades had been harmless sheets of metal faced with mirrors. Now they glinted evilly, as they revolved; the cold, cruel glint of keenly sharpened steel!

Straight toward this startling exhibit the Professor led the way, and as they approached Wentworth saw that his hunch had been right. The mirror-covered blades had been removed—and in their places *had* been fastened great blades of glinting, razor-sharp steel! Blades that revolved hungrily, yearningly—as if anxious for something upon which to feed!

Suspended above them was the grist that was ready to be dropped into the blades—human grist hanging by ropes through a circular opening in the ceiling immediately above the exhibit. Wentworth's pulses pounded, hot blood surging through his veins. Hanging over that hellish contraption, ropes tied around their waists, were more than a dozen men and women— amongst them, Nita!

With clenched fists Wentworth whirled on Thrall. But the Professor had stepped safely out of reach, where he now stood admiring his hell-inspired abomination.

"Tie him up!" he ordered.

The blank-faced men pulled Wentworth's hands behind his back, lashed them, then tied his ankles together securely.

"That is better," Thrall commended. "Now you are not likely to become too excited and attempt something rash. I see you *do* know Miss van Sloan, Wentworth. Excellent! You remember I promised you that this little party would be a reunion? Undoubtedly you will recognize other old friends among our dangling guests. They are the city's foremost busybodies and persecutors; people who cannot leave a man alone once he has served his time in a filthy penitentiary!"

For a moment the chuckling satisfaction was gone from his

manner, and the sensitive face darkened, became shrouded with bitter hatred. But then, as he saw Wentworth gazing up at the helpless victims, his diabolical good humor returned.

"Yes, you are right, Wentworth," he bobbed his head. "That one so close to your Miss van Sloan is Maida, my daughter—a brainless fool who has caused me sufficient trouble by running around and begging people to interfere in my affairs. She was so anxious to enlist Miss van Sloan's aid for my redemption—now she can die with her!"

NOT ONLY Nita and Maida Thrall did Wentworth recognize. Hanging there were prominent men and women who had disappeared mysteriously during the terror of the Green Death—wealthy people who must have been bled white by this sadistic madman. And among them, a haggard, listless figure who could scarcely hold up his head, was Howard Spalding, the erstwhile assistant who had promised to watch the professor and see that he did no harm!

"My redemption!" Thrall said savagely. "Of course, I am crazy—you know that, don't you, Wentworth? But if I am crazy it is your precious law that made me so!—Your precious, crooked law that sends an innocent man to jail and allows thieves and murderers to run at large. I was innocent of the charge on which they framed me and railroaded me to prison, Wentworth; I want you to know that before you die. It was that miserable creature hanging there, my faithful Spalding, who was the guilty one.

"Why did he betray me? For money, of course. Because he knew that my experiments had reached the point where he could cash in on them and reap a fortune. I was in his way! So he removed me by murdering half a dozen poor half-wits and planting the blame so that it would be placed at my door. Yes, Howard Spalding! With my own money he made an infamous deal with Franklin Penney, the prosecutor; a deal that bought his own immunity and consigned me to six years in a miserable cell!

"For more than six years I have waited patiently for the day when I would be able to square my account with those two gentlemen. Now that day is at hand. Franklin Penney is already doomed. One of my dependable assistants dropped a Green Death wafer into the carafe of water he drank at the Metropolitan Casino tonight. He thinks that he is robbing me of my percentage of the money he is making in my name. But the Green Death will collect from him, and that before this night is out. Now let us attend to our dear Spalding!"

He clapped his hands. Out onto a high platform, in the midst of the machinery that operated the mower, stepped an exotically caparisoned individual who looked like a Chinese fiend fresh from the pages of melodrama. A snarling-faced, long-mustached and goateed individual in flowing silken garments with a mandarin cap perched on his bald head. In his hand he held a long, sharp Oriental sword.

That man was no Oriental. Wentworth was sure of that almost instantly. To make certain, he shot a line of sing-song Cantonese at the fellow—and saw that it brought not the slightest response; not even a subconscious flicker of understanding. Wentworth stared hard—and knew the answer. That fellow was one of the blank-faced men in a Chinese make-up and costume.

Thrall's cracked brain evidently figured that it would add to the terror of his victims!

But his costume and make-up were as far as the fellow's make-believe went; the rest of his performance was all too genuine.

"Spalding," the gloating old man commanded—and that gleaming knife licked out and cut at the rope from which the dazed assistant hung suspended.

The rope severed, and Howard Spalding plunged downward into those steadily revolving knives. Hungrily they seized his body, sliced into it; fed it inside the ghastly machine, where other knives moving in the opposite direction completed the fearful work. As the sharp edges bit into him the dazed victim roused from his semi-coma and screamed in agony. Only for a few seconds... then he had disappeared entirely and the edges of the sharp blades were running with crimson....

"Brewster." Thrall called the name of another victim—and the long knife reached out to sever the rope which held the daughter of one of New York's wealthiest millionaires. Down into the terrible maw of the machine she plunged.

Endicott, McManus, Wilberforce, Terhuns... one after the other the demoniacal oldster called their names, and they were fed into the death machine. Richard Wentworth could do nothing but sit on the floor and watch. Each time those thin lips opened, he expected to hear the fiend intone "Van Sloan." But Thrall held that off, reveling in the torture he knew the suspense was inflicting....

Desperately Wentworth strained at the ropes, forgetting the

doom that hung over him. His struggle was hopeless. The rope was strong, the knots securely tied. It would take long hours to make any impression upon his bonds, and now perhaps even less than minutes remained. Frantically he attacked the knots again, tugged at the ropes until his wrists were raw and bleeding… and in the midst of his struggle suddenly the lights went out and the hall plunged into complete darkness.

Was this some more of Stephen Thrall's deviltry? Wentworth tried to peer through the blackness; tried to discover what new horror was about to descend upon him. A cold trickle ran through his spine as he felt somebody at his back! Somebody who hissed for silence—and slashed away at his ropes!

This was none of Thrall's doing. The Professor was yelling and cursing, shouting for lights… and now matches and a few flashlights were beginning to flicker and penetrate the gloom. His hands free, Wentworth snatched his own flashlight, snapped it on, whirled and turned it on his liberator—and was amazed to see that the beam was playing on the face of Stephen Thrall!

Stephen Thrall—and there, leaping toward him with a gun in his hand, was *another* Stephen Thrall!

BUT NOW the puzzle pieces were entirely in place. In a flash he understood the meaning of that amazing duplication, and he knew what to expect!

The Stephen Thrall of the demoniacal face came charging at him with murder in his eye. Wentworth crouched, ready to meet him. But just as they were about to clash, Wentworth's hand suddenly flashed to his throat, clutched at it wildly. A groan of agony ebbed from his lips, and his knees began to buckle beneath him—and just as he staggered he hurled himself forward, straight at the on-coming killer.

The Stephen Thrall who had liberated him—alike in every detail of dress and startlingly similar in face to the other—chose that same instant to leap upon his double. But the madman's automatic came down over his head and sent him reeling. Again the weapon rose to smash down over Wentworth's skull. Barely in time, Wentworth leaped aside. His fingers fastened on the man's gun-arm. He twisted. The gun dropped from the enraged killer's now nerveless fingers.

Man to man Wentworth closed with the fiend whom he had been trailing for weeks!

The battle which followed was strange indeed... A man beside himself with rage and hate, charging in savagely with flying fists and clawing, gouging fingers, pitted against one who could do nothing but retreat, could do nothing but hold his man off and watch for the opening that was his only chance. Half a dozen times Wentworth went down.

Each time he managed to squirm loose, managed to get back onto his feet and back away, watching every moment. Twice he almost secured the hold he wanted... and took a painful smash to the face when he missed. The third time his ravening opponent leaped full-tilt at him—and Wentworth's steely fingers fastened behind his left elbow, his arm slipped behind the fellow's back. There was hardly any exertion to what followed, but the body of the gray-haired fiend suddenly rose in the air in a backflip and landed on his face—in a fall guaranteed to break his neck!

Instantly Wentworth was upon him… but there was no more necessity for fighting; that grip had not failed. The fallen man was dying, his face was curiously distorted. His prominent nose had mushroomed horribly, was falling away in what looked like rotted flesh but was only facial modeling clay. Swiftly Wentworth tore away what remained of it, felt beneath the over-long gray hair until he found the almost imperceptible line he sought. He tore away the wig that covered a partially bald head. With cream from his own make-up kit he daubed the still face—and uncovered the features of Howard Spalding!

The real Howard Spalding this time; not the poor, brainless dupe whose face had been mutilated and changed until it was almost a duplicate of that of the fiend!

Even before that surprising revelation Wentworth had known what to expect. As he had lain there, watching the terrible operation of the death-machine, his understanding of Spalding's murderous trickery had become complete. Howard Spalding, expert surgeon and master of make-up—it had been easy for him to keep in touch with Thrall by visiting the prison in company with Maida; easy for him to watch the old man and note every change in him so that he was ready to counterpart him perfectly the moment the professor was released.

By perverting his profession in some devilish fashion, he had managed to get hold of these blank-faced men. When they were not blank-faced, he had operated on them fiendishly, while in the guise of Professor Thrall. He had made them believe that it was Thrall who was responsible for their suffering; Thrall from whom they took all orders. Then his preparations were complete.

All that remained was to wait for Thrall to be released from prison. Then he would spring the coup of the Green Death—the coup that would make him a huge fortune in criminal tribute!

What Spalding had told to his captives was all true—except that *he* was not the Thrall who had been wronged and railroaded to prison!

IT WAS Nita's scream that snapped Wentworth back to a realization that the battle was not over. Whirling, he saw with astonishment that the fellow up there on the machine platform, even without orders, was going ahead with his deadly work; grinning with mad delight as he cut loose another victim and dropped her into the whirling knives!

The other blank-faced men had gathered around the machine to revel in the orgy!

Wentworth saw that they were entirely out of hand. They had seen the man they knew as Professor Thrall killed, and now their fear of him was gone. They were free—free to disport themselves as horribly as their warped brains suggested. Poor, half-crazed victims of Spalding's fiendishness, no threat would halt them. The platform, where the pseudo-Chinese sat was too high to be reached from the floor. With that wicked knife, he would be able to drive back anyone who tried to climb up.

But there must be a way to reach that madman and stop him! The ceiling… Could Wentworth get up there above the circular opening through which the illumination had been turned on the exhibit below? At the far corner of the hall, a doorway which led to the executive offices… and perhaps to the electric light controls!

Wentworth raced to it, cast his flash beam around the dark offices. He found a doorway that led beyond to a ladder. This ran up the wall to the catwalks above the ceiling. Frantically, he threaded his way through that maze of little pathways, circling the openings in his way until he reached one above the death-machine. Now there were only three victims suspended over it—and the crazed knife-wielder was reaching out for the rope that held Nita!

It was too late to try to pull her up to safety—even if Wentworth had been able to reach the rope now far out in the opening. No time for that. Time now only to play his last card—to try to frighten that madman. As he hurried along the catwalks, Wentworth's fingers had been busy with his makeup materials.

From their concealment came the black cape, floppy-brimmed hat—the Spider was ready for the most desperate gamble of his career. Whipping out the silken cord from around his waist, he fastened it to a stanchion. Hand over hand he went down that slim line, penduluming himself as he descended. From his lipless gash of a mouth burst the eerie, maniacal cackle that was the Spider's laugh.

But for once that terrifying sound failed. It served only to spur the fellow with the knife. Seeing his prey about to be snatched from him, he snarled savagely—leaning far out from his seat to where Nita, unconscious, dangled limply. The knife reached her rope, sawed back and forth—and the strands parted!

Nita's body plummeted toward the hungry knives—and at that instant the Spider swung out, stretched forth, and grasped her in his arms!

Her weight was almost more than his half-crippled arm would bear. For a moment it seemed that she must slip away, must drop to her death. He clung, beads of perspiration on his forehead.

There was no chance whatever for him to climb back with her to the opening above. The snarling madman was leaning far out from his platform, making vicious swipes at the silken rope. One swift stroke of that keen blade, and both would plunge down to a ghastly death!

With all his strength, Wentworth urged his body with the diminishing arc of his pendulum swings. He strained every muscle to keep going, to increase the arc until he would swing out beyond the reach of those greedy blades. The arc was increasing....

And then the shriek of police whistles cut into his ears! The police were outside, clamoring at the doors of the hall. He could hear the blank-faced men trying to stop them—hear the pound of clubs and axes on the splintering doors. Now he heard Jim Mack's voice shouting to the men, calling to them to follow him. Jim Mack—still on the trail of the Spider! And now he would snare his man in full makeup!

SICK AND wounded, with death below and above him and with doom closing in from the distant doorway, the Spider was at the end of his resources. Hopelessly he looked upward— and saw the silken rope severed! Desperately he threw himself forward—hardly daring to glance down at the hungry knives that seemed to reach out greedy tentacles for his body and Nita's.

They were close, terribly close... they sliced into his black cape as his body skimmed past!

Then his body hit the floor with stunning force. For an instant everything went black and he thought that he was going to lose consciousness. But he fought stubbornly... fought back to a fresh grip on his senses. Groggily he got to his knees, then his feet. Thank God... Nita seemed uninjured.

The noise of the advancing police drummed into Wentworth's brain. Nita was all right now. Thrall was a physician, and he would look after her. The blank-faced men were all up at the front of the hall, trying to stop the police or frantically seeking a place to hide themselves.

In a few moments the police would be swarming into the hall; Jim Mack would be there to seize him. Before that time, he must be gone. Yes, Wentworth must be gone... but the Spider could still be here to appease that bloodhound.

Already a plan had taken shape in his mind. Grabbing Spalding's unconscious body, he dragged it behind another large machinery exhibit and went to work on it. Quickly he changed clothes with the corpse and made up the dead face in a replica of Casimir Belotti's. Inside Belotti's coat he hid the Spider's cape and hat, his straggly wig and his makeup kit articles that would identify the corpse absolutely as the Spider's.

Now let Jim Mack come in with his police and find the Spider! Let him find the dead body of Casimir Belotti, the street musician whom he was so sure was the other self of Blinky McQuade and of the Spider!

The police were racing across the hall, lighting it with their flashes, as Richard Wentworth found a side door far in the rear. He slipped quietly into the dark, empty grounds of the World's Fair.

Now Casimir Belotti was gone; gone with Blinky McQuade and with Richard Wentworth and with the Spider. One more useful work was finished. Like a cat he had shed his lives, Wentworth realized; and now once more he had risen phoenix-like from the ashes of a personality that had served him well. But how long could he keep on doing that?

Those were questions about which it was better not to think...

A chill coursed down the length of his spine as he slunk between the ghostly buildings. In that moment, Richard Wentworth was a very lonesome man—lonesome for Nita, for Jackson, for Ram Singh, for the friends and comforts that were any man's right and that seemed to be barred forever from the life of the Spider....

THE SPIDER

- ❏ #1: The Spider Strikes — $13.95
- ❏ #2: The Wheel of Death — $13.95
- ❏ #3: Wings of the Black Death — $13.95
- ❏ #4: City of Flaming Shadows — $13.95
- ❏ #5: Empire of Doom! — $13.95
- ❏ #6: Citadel of Hell — $13.95
- ❏ #7: The Serpent of Destruction — $13.95
- ❏ #8: The Mad Horde — $13.95
- ❏ #9: Satan's Death Blast — $13.95
- ❏ #10: The Corpse Cargo — $13.95
- ❏ #11: Prince of the Red Looters — $13.95
- ❏ #12: Reign of the Silver Terror — $13.95
- ❏ #13: Builders of the Dark Empire — $13.95
- ❏ #14: Death's Crimson Juggernaut — $13.95
- ❏ #15: The Red Death Rain — $13.95
- ❏ #16: The City Destroyer — $13.95
- ❏ #17: The Pain Emperor — $13.95
- ❏ #18: The Flame Master — $13.95
- ❏ #19: Slaves of the Crime Master — $13.95
- ❏ #20: Reign of the Death Fiddler — $13.95
- ❏ #21: Hordes of the Red Butcher — $13.95
- ❏ #22: Dragon Lord of the Underworld — $13.95
- ❏ #23: Master of the Death-Madness — $13.95
- ❏ #24: King of the Red Killers — $13.95
- ❏ #25: Overlord of the Damned — $13.95
- ❏ #26: Death Reign of the Vampire King — $13.95
- ❏ #27: Emperor of the Yellow Death — $13.95
- ❏ #28: The Mayor of Hell — $13.95
- ❏ #29: Slaves of the Murder Syndicate — $13.95
- ❏ #30: Green Globes of Death — $13.95
- ❏ #31: The Cholera King — $13.95
- ❏ #32: Slaves of the Dragon — $13.95
- ❏ #33: Legions of Madness — $12.95
- ❏ #34: Laboratory of the Damned — $12.95
- ❏ #35: Satan's Sightless Legion — $12.95
- ❏ #36: The Coming of the Terror — $12.95
- ❏ #37: The Devil's Death-Dwarfs — $12.95
- ❏ #38: City of Dreadful Night — $12.95
- ❏ #39: Reign of the Snake Men — $12.95
- ❏ #40: Dictator of the Damned — $12.95
- ❏ #41: The Mill-Town Massacres — $12.95
- ❏ #42: Satan's Workshop — $12.95
- ❏ #43: Scourge of the Yellow Fangs — $12.95
- ❏ #44: The Devil's Pawnbroker — $12.95
- ❏ #45: Voyage of the Coffin Ship — $12.95
- ❏ #46: The Man Who Ruled in Hell — $13.95
- ❏ #47: Slaves of the Black Monarch — $13.95
- ❏ #48: Machineguns Over the White House — $13.95
- ❏ #49: The City That Dared Not Eat — $13.95
- ❏ #50: Master of the Flaming Horde — $13.95
- ❏ #51: Satan's Switchboard — $13.95
- ❏ #52: Legions of the Accursed Light — $13.95
- ❏ #53: The City of Lost Men — $13.95
- ❏ #54: The Grey Horde Creeps — $13.95
- ❏ #55: City of Whispering Death — $13.95
- ❏ #56: When Thousands Slept in Hell — $13.95
- ❏ #57: Satan's Shakles — $14.95
- ❏ #58: The Emperor From Hell — $14.95
- ❏ #59: The Devil's Candlesticks — $14.95
- ❏ #60: The City That Paid to Die — $14.95
- ❏ #61: The Spider at Bay — $14.95
- ❏ #62: Scourge of the Black Legions — $14.95
- ❏ #63: The Withering Death — $14.95
- ❏ #64: Claws of the Golden Dragon — $14.95
- ❏ #65: The Song of Death — $14.95
- ❏ #66: The Silver Death Reign — $14.95
- ❏ #67: Blight of the Blazing Eye — $14.95
- ❏ #68: King of the Fleshless Legion — $14.95
- ❏ #69: Rule of the Monster Men — $16.95
- ❏ #70: The Spider and the Slaves of Hell — $16.95
- ❏ #71: The Spider and the Fire God — $16.95
- ❏ ***NEW:*** #72: The Corpse Broker — $16.95

THE WESTERN RAIDER

- ❏ #1: Guns of the Damned — $13.95
- ❏ #2: The Hawk Rides Back from Death — $13.95
- ❏ #3: Gun-Call for the Lost Legion — $13.95
- ❏ #4: The Law of Silver Trent — $13.95
- ❏ #5: The Gun-Prayer of Silver Trent — $13.95
- ❏ #6: Silver Trent Rides Alone — $13.95

G-8 AND HIS BATTLE ACES

- ❏ #1: The Bat Staffel — $13.95

CAPTAIN SATAN

- ❏ #1: The Mask of the Damned — $13.95
- ❏ #2: Parole for the Dead — $13.95
- ❏ #3: The Dead Man Express — $13.95
- ❏ #4: A Ghost Rides the Dawn — $13.95
- ❏ #5: The Ambassador From Hell — $13.95

DR. YEN SIN

- ❏ #1: Mystery of the Dragon's Shadow — $12.95
- ❏ #2: Mystery of the Golden Skull — $12.95
- ❏ #3: Mystery of the Singing Mummies — $12.95

RED FINGER

- ❏ #1: Second-Hand Death — $24.95